The Diary of Valaryn Syldanor

A Simple Housemaid from the Freelands

Written & Illustrated
By Maruse Rino

Also by Maruse Rino:

Night of the Werewolves

Tristaria Volume 1

The Diary of Valaryn Syldanor
A Simple Housemaid from the Freelands

1st Edition

© Maruse Rino 2022

ISBN: 978-0-6450787-2-5

Greetings to you, who are reading this. My name is Valaryn Syldanor. I am not an important person, by any measure, so you may wonder why it is that I have decided to put down my thoughts and experiences in this little notebook. The truth is that I only decided upon doing this today. You see, today is my eighteenth birthday, and my kindly mistress, Mrs Greyfield, gifted me this fine notebook and suggested I use it to practice my writing skills.

When I first started working at Greyfield Manor, I could neither read nor write. I have managed to teach myself to read over this time, mainly by reading children's stories to my Aunt Tilumina, but writing has proven a more difficult challenge. So I think Mrs Greyfield's suggestion is a good one. However, simply writing for the sake of practice hardly fills me with any enthusiasm, so that is why I came up with the idea of keeping a diary. I will endeavour to write in it as often as I can, but as I explained earlier, I am not an important person, which means I generally do not have anything particularly interesting to write about. Furthermore, I am quite busy and have very little time for myself. So you must forgive me if my diary ends up being very dull and very short, but today, at least, I have quite a lot to write about.

To begin with, perhaps I should tell you a bit more about myself. I am a Freelander. I was born in the Freelands, the same as my mother. My father, however, was from the Oldlands. To be more specific, he was from Alfynlund, the ancient land of the elves. Apparently, my father was from a wealthy family, and in his youth, his relatives had arranged for him to marry a noblewoman. Although my father had no special feelings for this noblewoman, he was happy to go along with this arrangement, if only to please his relatives. But then something unexpected happened. He met my mother.

My mother, who was from a common Freelander family, had shown a great talent for painting from a very young age, and thus had managed to attain a scholarship to study at a prestigious art school in Valys, the capital city of Alfynlund. When my mother and father met, they fell madly in love with one another (or they both simply went mad, as Aunt Tilu likes to tell me), and they eloped. My mother abandoned her studies, and my father turned his back on his family. They settled down in the town of Drylake, in the southern Freelands, where I was born. However, my mother soon took ill, and passed away.

My father took my mother's death quite badly, and within a year of her passing, he chose to end his own life by throwing himself into the sea. That left me in the care of Aunt Tilu. She took me to the northeast with her, to the city of New Rondir, where she took good care of me. But alas, in time the malady that took my mother also descended upon my aunt, so when I turned fifteen, I went to work as a housemaid in the house of a local noble family, the Greyfields. Now, I do my best to look after her, just as she looked after me when I was small.

I have now been working for the Greyfields for nearly three years. Generally, the work is long and tiring, but the Greyfields are a wonderful family, and they treat everyone with such great kindness. For example, Mrs Greyfield makes a point of celebrating the birthday of every single member of the household, including the servants. And so it was that Lady Greyfield asked the other maids to organise a little party for me, which was held earlier this evening. Just about everybody in the household was at this party. Mrs Greyfield was present, of course, as were her five children. And all the other servants were there too (or at least, I should say, the ones who had been rostered for today were). In fact, the only notable absence was the head of the household, Mr Greyfield himself. But there was a good reason for that. For the past few weeks, he has been away on business in the Oldlands. According to Mrs Greyfield, it had been his intention to return in time for my little party, but alas, there has been a lot of unrest in the Oldlands lately (rumours of imminent war abound), and his ship was late in departing, so he won't be back until next week.

Apart from the notebook from Mrs Greyfield, I received other fine presents, but amongst these there were two that really stood out. The first was a lovely frock from Eliara (one of my fellow housemaids), who made it herself. I shall be sure to wear it once the weather improves (it is still quite cold here in New Rondir). The second was the present from the cook. He prepared his famous fruit and nut cake, which I like tremendously. We all shared it with some tea. But I made sure to save a piece for dear Aunt Tilu. She was already asleep when I got home, so I will give it to her for breakfast tomorrow. I'm sure she'll enjoy it.

Today seemed to be a rather relaxed day (due partly to the party, I suspect), but very soon, things will doubtlessly become very busy at Greyfield Manor, as we all begin preparing for Mr Greyfield's imminent return. But despite that, I'm really looking forward to seeing Mr Greyfield again. He always brings us servants a little souvenir (usually a tasty sweet of some kind) and, in addition, he always has interesting tales to tell about his travels.

The past couple of days have been incredibly busy. As I wrote last time, this was because Mrs Greyfield wanted the house to look magnificent before Mr Greyfield came home, and look magnificent it did. However, it was quite late when Mr Greyfield arrived, and he was so exhausted that he retired to his room almost immediately. So I don't think he would have noticed the efforts of all the household till he awoke the following morning.

As usual, Mr Greyfield had gifts for everyone. But on top of that, he had an extra special gift for me. This was, as Mr Greyfield put it, a "somewhat belated birthday present". It was a handmade dish, which had been decorated with a painting of Mount Miron in Alfynlund (my father had been born in a town near this mountain). I'm grateful for Mr Greyfield going to the trouble of getting me this gift, but to be honest, I do not really know what I should do with it. It seems too nice to eat from it, but I don't really have a place in my room to display it either, so perhaps I shall give it to my aunt. After all, she has actually seen Mount Miron, unlike me. Of more interest to me was the many newspapers Mr Greyfield brought back from the Oldlands, in particular those from Alfynlund. Mr Greyfield let me borrow a few of them and I spent most of last night looking through them.

Most of the news from the Oldlands is depressing. The threat of war in the Oldlands seems to grow daily. In fact, only last week, an assassin managed to murder the last direct heir to the Alfynlundic crown, Prince Uldryc, who was going to become king in March. The prince's assassin, a young Alfynlundic man, was captured, but he somehow managed to do away with himself before he could be questioned thoroughly. A few of the newspapers assumed the young man was merely a crazed anarchist, but most seemed to believe he was actually working as an agent for the Troluskan government. That is hardly surprising, as the nations of Alfynlund and Troluska have had bad relations for many, many years now. I do not pretend to fully understand what is behind this longstanding animosity, but it seems to me that, as ridiculous as it sounds, it stems from disputes that took place several centuries ago.

On a side note, as a result of the crown prince's death, there is now a succession crisis in Alfynlund. The Royal Council of Alfynlund (which is made up of the six most senior officials in all of Alfynlund, which includes the prime minister and the hundred-and-one-year-old head of the Church of Alfynlund, Lord Galyrod), will soon be convening to choose a successor to the crown. Since there are no direct heirs left, the council is expected to choose a nobleman or noblewoman with some connection to the royal family in the not-so-distant past.

Next week, all of us at Greyfield Manor will be very busy once again. I forgot to mention this before, but the reason Mr Greyfield had been abroad was to finalise the arrangements for his eldest son's entry into a prestigious university in Alfynlund. With all the problems in the Oldlands at present, I personally don't think going to Alfynlund is a very good idea, and I have the suspicion Mrs Greyfield agrees with me. But the young master is determined to see the world, as it were, and he has the full support of his father.

This has been a rather trying week. Not only was Greyfield Manor in a frenzy for several days until the young master left to go and study abroad, but a few days ago my poor aunt's health took a sudden turn for the worst as well. And then, just today, a most surprising thing occurred!

Everyone in the Greyfield household was sad when young Master Pelton departed. He is an incredibly charming young man, and there were quite a number of tears shed, especially by his mother, who could hardly keep her eyes dry. Even Mr Greyfield looked unusually nervous, as if he suddenly regretted having agreed to send his son to the Oldlands. In fact, the only one who looked at all happy was the young master himself. He had a great big smile when I saw him last, waving from the window of the carriage that was to take him to the docks. I truly hope for his sake that things in Alfynlund do not get any worse than they already are, but something deep inside me tells me this is a vain hope.

According to the doctor who called in to see my aunt the other day, my aunt is in need of specialist care that could only be provided at the main city hospital. That is out of the question for us at the moment, unfortunately, as the money I have been saving for this purpose is still not enough. But I am sure that by the time winter sets in it will be. Mrs Greyfield, who is genuinely concerned about my aunt's health, has on numerous occasions offered to lend me the money for the hospital. However, whenever I have mentioned this to my aunt, she has always balked at the idea. She thinks it would be terrible for me to get into debt at such a young age. But should my aunt's health worsen any further, I shall certainly give Mrs Greyfield's offer serious consideration.

And what of the surprising occurrence I mentioned at the beginning of this entry? That was a strange letter addressed to my late father from the Alfynlundic Embassy. The letter stated that the Alfynlundic ambassador himself wished to discuss an important matter with my father in relation to his family. However, the letter gave no indication of what this important matter might be. It merely suggested that it was something too sensitive to put down in writing. When I showed that letter to my aunt, she was suspicious. The embassy, she reasoned, would never send out letters to someone without checking if that someone was still alive. I decided she was right and so I disposed of the letter without a second thought.

Poor Auntie!

January 23rd, 137 FC

Well, what a surprise I had today! Upon leaving my apartment early this morning to go to work, I was approached by a rather scary-looking gentleman dressed in garb that I recognised as the military uniform of Alfynlund. Actually, the only scary-looking thing about the gentleman was that he wore an eyepatch over his left eye, and that he had a long scar running down his left cheek, which seemed to me to have been recently acquired. His manner was terribly polite, and he introduced himself as Captain Ulryf Keldaron, of the Alfynlundic Royal Guard, although he had come to my apartment as a representative of the Alfynlundic Embassy.

Once he had finished with his introduction, Captain Keldaron asked if I knew the whereabouts of Ormyl Syldanor (my father). I was already running late for work, so I told the captain I had no time to speak with him and I walked away. However, I did let it slip that I was Ormyl's daughter, so it was hardly surprising that when I left Greyfield Manor later that day, Captain Keldaron was waiting for me outside the gate. I told him I had nothing more to say to him and that if he continued to follow me around, I would call the police. Unfortunately, this failed to dissuade him, but thankfully Mrs Greyfield became aware of what was happening, and she came out to confront the captain.

Mrs Greyfield demanded Captain Keldaron prove that he was indeed a representative of the Alfynlundic Embassy, as he claimed he was, and the captain obediently produced his documentation. After looking over the papers, Mrs Greyfield seemed satisfied the captain was telling the truth, and he asked the captain what he was doing in the Freelands. The captain was elusive in his response, but he did state that he was here to speak to Ormyl Syldanor about a very important family matter. When Mrs Greyfield told him Ormyl was deceased, the captain looked a little taken aback, but he quickly recovered and, addressing me, asked if it was true that I was his daughter. I said yes, and the captain went on to ask if I had any siblings. I said no.

After taking a moment to do some pondering, Captain Keldaron asked me if I would be willing to meet with the ambassador. At my earliest convenience, of course. I replied that I worked six days a week, and on my days off I had many things to do. However, at that point Mrs Greyfield kindly offered to let me have a day off early next week, so that I might go to the embassy and see what all this fuss was about. The captain seemed pleased with this outcome. I myself am not altogether happy with the idea of taking a long, dull trip into town, but I do admit I am just a little bit curious about this mysterious "important family matter". In any case, I do hope things will be cleared up quickly.

Incidentally, as I am writing this, I have the curious feeling that I've met Captain Keldaron before somewhere, although I cannot imagine under what circumstance that could have been. After all, I am sure that I have never met a soldier from Alfynlund in all my life. It is another little mystery, and perhaps it too will be solved next week.

How may
I help you?

January 28th, 137 FC

Well, I do not know quite where to begin. Today, I went to the Alfynlundic Embassy, and as a result, my life has been completely turned upside-down. It turns out that I am royalty! But I am getting too far ahead of myself. Let me go back to the start of the day.

After I awoke this morning, I got dressed in the clothes I usually wear when I go to work. I did this because I decided it was best not to tell Aunt Tilu what my plans were for today. And besides, I would not know how to dress for a visit to an embassy anyway.

To keep up the charade that it was just another workday for me, I left my apartment quite early, but this was to my benefit. This allowed me to walk to the nearest train station, instead of catching a carriage, which saved me a bit of money. The train ticket into town on its own is very expensive!

I arrived at the Alfynlundic Embassy with quite a bit of time to spare, and for a moment I thought about walking around town for a while, to pass the time. But I am unfamiliar with the city, as I have visited it only a handful of times in the past, and there was a good chance that if I started wandering around its numerous winding lanes, I would very quickly become lost. So I found a bench in a nearby park to sit on, until the time of my appointment arrived.

The Alfynlundic Embassy is a beautiful old stone building, but it's very small, so when I was shown into the ambassador's office by the ambassador's personal secretary, I was rather surprised to find it incredibly spacious. It did not have a lot of furniture, but what furniture it did have was all impeccably clean and antique-looking. The ambassador, a well-dressed, short and plump middle-aged man, was evidently very pleased to see me. Captain Keldaron, who was also present and dressed once again in his military uniform, looked relieved more than anything else. I suppose he had been concerned that I might not show up for the meeting at all. After we all exchanged greetings, the ambassador asked me if I had heard about the recent tragedy that involved the crown prince of Alfynlund. I told him that I had, and that was when I realised why Captain Keldaron's face had seemed familiar to me. His face, still wrapped in fresh bandages, had been clearly printed in one of the newspapers I had borrowed from Mr Greyfield. Indeed, when I spoke to him for the first time, he had told me he was a member of the Alfynlundic Royal Guard, but only at the embassy did I make the connection to the crown prince's assassination. Captain Keldaron had most likely been travelling quite close to the crown prince's carriage on that fateful day.

The ambassador then went on to explain to me that the Kingdom of Alfynlund was in dire need of finding a suitable heir to the now vacant throne, and that I, through my father, was one of several possible candidates. I nearly fell out of my chair when I heard this. There had never been any mention of royal lineage in my family before. I suggested to the ambassador that he must have gotten our family mixed up with another. But he insisted there was no mistake, as it had been recently determined that one of my father's grandparents was in fact the illegitimate offspring of King Thuryc IV.

I still could not believe what I was hearing, but I patiently listened to what this supposedly meant for me.

The Alfynlundic government was prepared to pay me (handsomely) to travel to Alfynlund and undertake an intensive training course in royal etiquette, and if it was determined that I was the most suitable of the candidates, I would be recognised as a member of the royal family. After that, I would receive special training for a special ceremony that was due to take place in Alfynlund in the middle of summer. He did not say much concerning this ceremony, other than it was an ancient tradition that would serve as a much-needed morale boost for the people of Alfynlund in these dark times. But first I needed to consent to all of this.

It was clear from their expressions that both the ambassador and the captain expected me to agree to this royal proposal right there and then, but that was impossible. I told them it was a big decision for me and that I needed at least a week to think things over carefully. In the end they both agreed with me, albeit rather reluctantly.

After I left the embassy, I found myself walking about the city in a bit of a daze. But eventually (and by sheer luck) I came upon a train station. From there, I headed straight back home. When I got to my apartment, however, it was not long after noon, so I was forced to tell my aunt that I had been allowed to leave work early because I had felt unusually tired. I'm not sure she believed me, but thankfully she did not question me. Now I just have to work out the best way to tell her the truth.

It took me until today to work up the courage to tell Aunt Tilu about what had really happened the day I came home early. At first, she was understandably angry that I had deceived her and disregarded her advice, but she quickly calmed down and said that since I was no longer a child, she could not force me to do anything. Yet even as she said this, I could see that she was merely putting on a brave face for my sake, and that the truth was that she was afraid of being left alone, with no-one to take care of her. This broke my heart, and I promised my aunt at once that I would not be leaving her for any reason.

To be honest, I was actually a little bit excited at the thought of visiting Alfynlund. Even with the threat of war looming over it, it would have been nice to be able to go there and perhaps visit the places my father and my mother frequented. I might even have been able to visit some of my Alfynlundic relatives (if, of course, they weren't opposed to my doing so). However, as I mentioned to Mrs Greyfield when she asked me about my visit to the embassy, deep down in my heart I just know that I am not really of royal blood. Although I lost my father at a very young age, I was very close to him, and I believe I knew him quite well. Despite having turned his back on his family, he remained extremely proud of his heritage, and he often entertained me with tales of his youth in Alfynlund. Not once had he mentioned that we were connected to the royal family of Alfynlund in any way. Not once.

I will have to leave this entry in my diary here, as short as it has been, for now I need to write a letter to the ambassador and politely decline his kind offer. I'll try to make it as brief as possible, so I can finish it before I go to bed tonight. That way, I'll be able to post it first thing in the morning, and therefore it should reach the embassy within the time I promised the ambassador.

Scritchity-
Scratch

17

Today most certainly has been another eventful day in the life of Valaryn Syldanor, the simple housemaid. I had not expected to hear from the Alfynlundic Embassy ever again, so I was quite surprised when, upon leaving Greyfield Manor this evening, I saw a rather magnificent carriage waiting outside the gate, with the emblem of the Alfynlundic government painted on the door. However, it was not the ambassador who was in it. It was Captain Keldaron, dressed smartly, as always, in his military uniform.

I told the captain at once that I had neither the time nor any reason to speak with him. I was not going to Alfynlund and that was that. But the captain was merely keen to know why I had declined his government's offer. Admittedly, I had not provided any explanation for my decision in the letter I sent to the ambassador (which may have ended up being a little bit too brief), so I suppose it was a reasonable enquiry. But I needed to get home to prepare dinner for my aunt and myself. Captain Keldaron then offered to take me home on the embassy carriage, proposing that I explain the reasoning behind my decision to him on the way there. I accepted his offer.

I told the captain about my aunt and her ailment in detail. He listened attentively. Once I had finished speaking, the captain thought for a long while, and then he offered me a deal. The Alfynlundic Embassy would see to it that my aunt received the best treatment available in New Rondir, for as long as it was needed. In return, all I had to do was agree to travel to Alfynlund and undertake the intensive training course. If, after I completed the course, I decided I did not want to stay in Alfynlund, I would be free to return home.

Well, this sounded like an altogether wonderful deal! So, needless to say, I was suspicious. I asked him why he was so invested in this grand plan to find a suitable heir to the Alfynlundic throne. The captain then told me (as I had already guessed), that he had been present when the crown prince had been assassinated. Apart from the great sense of shame this event had brought upon him, he was also filled with incredible grief, as the crown prince had been a close friend of his since childhood. As he spoke, I was surprised to see the captain weep openly. It was rare to see a man weep. It was rarer still to see a soldier do so. Therefore, I believe that his tears were genuine and that what he told me was true. But regardless of that, I still needed time to think things over. And, of course, I also needed to know what my aunt thought about this latest development. Therefore, in the end, I told the captain to meet me outside my apartment in the morning, at which time I would give him my final answer on this matter.

I waited until Aunt Tilu and I had finished eating dinner before I brought up Captain Keldaron's deal. By this time, I was leaning towards accepting his deal, mainly because of what this would mean for my aunt, and, accordingly, I had steeled myself for the challenge of convincing my aunt to agree with me. But in the end, I was the one who needed convincing. This was because the closer the idea of going to Alfynlund got to becoming reality, the more frightened I began to feel, and the more reasons I could think of for staying in New Rondir. And the foremost of these reasons was, of course, my aunt. If I agreed to go to Alfynlund, I would be there for at least three months before I could return to the Freelands. And what if my aunt's condition should worsen during that time?

When I said this to Aunt Tilu, she laughed, a good hearty laugh that was full of life, and she told me that she had no plans on leaving this world any time soon. In fact, she was determined to stay alive until I was at the very least happily married, so if I had decided that I wanted to go to Alfynlund, then I should go.

For some reason, my aunt's words filled me with a great sense of relief. I guess this is because even though I am no longer a child (as my aunt reminded me not too long ago), I do still feel like one at times. The idea of my getting married and the idea of Aunt Tilu no longer being around both seem like an eternity away right now.

This morning, as I had requested, Captain Keldaron was waiting for me outside my home, and I promptly informed him that I had decided to go to Alfynlund. He looked very pleased if not outright happy to hear this, and he suddenly started explaining to me all that I needed to do to prepare for the trip, in great detail. But I told him he was letting himself become overly excited, as I still needed to go to work. He laughed and said there was no need, as he could arrange a passage for me out of the Freelands tonight! I may have come across as being a little bit rude, but at this point I felt I needed to put my foot down. I told the captain quite clearly that I would not set foot on any ship, nor would I even go down to the docks, until Aunt Tilu was safely in hospital, as Captain Keldaron had promised she would be. Only then would I start preparing for the trip.

As you can imagine, this took the wind right out of the captain's sails, so to speak. But he quickly regrouped, and he said that he would start making the necessary arrangements so that my aunt could be admitted to the main city hospital within a week. I thought he was being incredibly optimistic, but we left it at that.

After I arrived at Greyfield Manor, I made sure to take a moment to speak to Mrs Greyfield before I started on my chores. I told her that I had decided to go to Alfynlund after all, and that I would be leaving her family's employment at the end of the week. I did not know how Mrs Greyfield would react to this news, but she seemed quite thrilled by the idea. I do recall hearing that Mrs

Greyfield had been quite adventurous in her younger days, so maybe she was excited for me.

Mrs Greyfield suggested a little farewell party, but I told her I would feel rather guilty at having had two parties held in my honour so soon after one another. I also told her, of course, that I was certain I would return to the Freelands sooner rather than later, and that I hoped I would be able to return to serve the Greyfield family when I did. Mrs Greyfield assured me that everyone would welcome me back with open arms, which made me very happy.

On my way home from work today, I absentmindedly took a slight detour, and I stopped on one of the major bridges spanning the Great Northern River, to watch the sun set. It was a beautiful sight, but it made me a little sad to think that in a week or so, I would be a long, long way from here, the place where I had spent most of my young life.

Right now, my heart is roiling with conflicting emotions. On the one hand, I feel overjoyed because Aunt Tilu was finally admitted into the main city hospital earlier today. On the other, I am devastated because I am leaving with Captain Keldaron for the Oldlands tomorrow morning, and I will be separated from my Aunt Tilu for the first time since my father died.

As I had anticipated, Aunt Tilu's hospital stay wasn't at all easy to arrange, but Captain Keldaron managed to do it in the end. Furthermore, he also managed to get my aunt a private room! I don't really know how much all this will cost the Alfynlundic Embassy, but it will be anything but cheap. I know this because last year I visited the very same city hospital in order to make inquiries on my aunt's behalf. At that time, I distinctly recall being thoroughly impressed by how clean and modern the hospital looked, but I very nearly fainted when I found out how much the hospital charged for its services.

After Aunt Tilu had settled into the hospital, I stayed with her as long as I could, and we talked about all sorts of silly, trivial things, just to keep ourselves from having to face up to the reality that I was going away for who knows how long. But eventually, of course, a nurse appeared to politely inform us that the time allowed for visitors was almost over. It was at that moment that I solemnly promised my aunt that upon completing my training course in Alfynlund, I would immediately come back to the Freelands, no matter what. Aunt Tilu wondered if it was wise for me to make such a promise without knowing exactly what the outcome of all this would be. But I told her there was only one possible outcome, and that was that I would be one of the first candidates the Royal Council of Alfynlund sent back home, probably in nothing more than a rowboat. My aunt and I both laughed at my little joke, but not for very long. Soon, we were both in each other's arms, sobbing and weeping.

After saying goodbye to Aunt Tilu, I went straight to the hospital's lobby, where Captain Keldaron was waiting for me. He handed me my ticket for passage to the Oldlands, and he told me that he had already arranged for a carriage to take me from my home down to the docks first thing in the morning. When I heard those words, the enormity of what I had agreed upon finally struck me. In my head, I desperately began thinking of all the things I still had to do before I could leave, but there weren't any. Everything that needed to be settled had been already settled.

After Aunt Tilu's welfare, my chief concern had been our apartment. So, a few days ago, I gave our landlord an advance payment of six months' rent, with the understanding that he would not lease the room to another soul while I was away. (In case you are wondering, I was able to pay for all this rent by using most of the money I had been putting aside for my aunt.) Captain Keldaron, however, was of the opinion that I was throwing my money away. He reasoned that if I did end up coming back to the Freelands in a few months' time, the Alfynlundic government would see to it that I was provided with a newer, much more spacious dwelling nearer to the hospital. But honestly, who could believe the Alfynlundic government would want anything to do with me once I was out of the Oldlands? And, what's more, I expect that my aunt's condition will be a whole lot better when I get back to New Rondir. Therefore, there won't be any need for me to live near the hospital.

The only other main concern I had was deciding what I needed to take to Alfynlund, but that proved to be a very simple task in the end. Captain Keldaron told me I only needed to pack enough belongings for the trip itself. Everything else would be provided for me in Alfynlund.

So, as you can see, there is nothing for me to use as an excuse to delay the inevitable. Captain Keldaron had kept his word regarding my aunt. Therefore, it is now my turn to keep mine.

As I write this, I am no longer in the Freelands. I am somewhere in the middle of the Great Dividing Ocean, on board an enormous passenger ship (named the GS Queen Kalvilaria III) that is steaming its way to the Oldlands. The GS stands for "Gomonian Ship", and from this information you may have deduced that this ship will not be travelling directly to Alfynlund. It will be stopping at the Kingdom of Gomonia first. Of course, Captain Keldaron would have much preferred to have travelled on a ship that went directly to Alfynlund, but unfortunately this was the best he could find at short notice. Our journey will therefore take a little longer than it normally would, but that does not seem to concern the captain. For him, the bigger problem is the size of the cabins. As you probably know, the people of Gomonia, the gnomes, are of rather small stature and their ships are built to match. Captain Keldaron, who is not, by any means, tall for an Alfynlundic gentleman, is like an eagle in a bird cage. No matter where he turns, he seems to bump into something. Fortunately, I do not have this problem. I have always had a small frame, so much so that I could easily pass for a tall Gomonian lady.

It will take roughly a week for us to arrive in Gomonia, so to stave off boredom, Captain Keldaron has begun to tell me a little of Alfynlundic history, which, despite being half-Alfynlundic myself, I know next to nothing about. In fact, just about the only thing I knew about this subject has to do with my name. You see, Valaryn is an old

Alfynlundic name. My father had once told me that it had been the name of an ancient Alfynlundic princess, one who had been dearly loved by the people of Alfynlund. But that was all I knew. Captain Keldaron explained to me that Princess Valaryn had saved Alfynlund by leading an army against an invasion from Troluska. He then remarked that when he had first been asked to travel to the Freelands in search of my father, he had never dreamed he would find a girl who was named after her. The way he said it made it seem as there was something fateful about our meeting.

Obviously, I choose to believe that it's nothing more than a coincidence. I certainly have no ambition to lead any sort of military operation against the Kingdom of Troluska (or any other country for that matter). All I expect to have to do in Alfynlund is learn to behave like a proper royal does. And that, for a simple housemaid like me at least, seems challenging enough.

We have arrived in Gomonia! That is the good news. The bad news is that poor weather has delayed the departure of GS Queen Kalvilaria III, for at least a couple of days. Accordingly, Captain Keldaron has decided that we should switch mode of transport and travel the remainder of the journey by train. In fact, as I write this, I am already aboard the train, which is currently speeding through the Gomonian countryside. From what I have heard, the rolling green hills of Gomonia are a sight to behold. Unfortunately, however, it is now night-time, so apart from the occasional dark silhouette of a tree, I can hardly see a thing. In fact, as far as enjoying the sights is concerned, my first day in the Oldlands has been, for the most part, disappointing. When, earlier today, the Queen Kalvilaria III berthed in Galimos (the westernmost port of Gomonia), I didn't get to see very much of it, because after leaving the docks we only had to cross a single road to arrive at the train terminus! But during that most brief and hurried walk (we were running late for the train), I did catch a glimpse of a few buildings, and they were quite lovely. The Gomonians have a great reputation as craftsmen, and this is quite evident in their buildings, which are all ornately decorated. Compared to the enormous buildings in the Freelands, however, they do seem rather diminutive.

On a side note, I found it interesting that unlike the Queen Kalvilaria III, the train we are on has been cleverly constructed to accommodate both gnomes and non-gnomes alike. The train's carriages are all the same height, but the ones at the front (the ones exclusively for gnomes) consist of two decks. The ones at the rear (the ones for non-gnomes) consist of only one. Needless to say, after the cramped quarters on the ship, Captain Keldaron is glad to be able to stretch his legs out without any risk of knocking anything or anybody over. But in any case, the journey will not be a terribly long one. Tomorrow morning, our train will cross Gomonia's eastern border and enter Alfynlund, and then it should reach Valys, the capital city of Alfynlund, in the early evening.

Right now, I am on the balcony of the spacious and extremely extravagant hotel room Captain Keldaron booked for me, somewhere in the heart of Valys. The sun set not so long ago, and below me the city streets are growing dim as the sky gradually darkens.

What, you may ask, are my impressions of Alfynlund, the land of my father's family, thus far? Well, to be honest I haven't seen a lot of it yet. When Captain Keldaron and I stepped off the train, we came straight here, to the hotel known as "The Grand Unicorn". But since the distance between the train station and the hotel was much too far to travel on foot, we took a carriage, and I used that opportunity to look around as much as I could.

At first glance, Valys appears quite similar to New Rondir. However, the streets are not so wide here, and there are hardly any tall buildings. Furthermore, it lacks the newness that New Rondir has in abundance. But I do not mean that this makes Valys unattractive. On the contrary, everything in it has a sort of vintage look to it, including such ordinary things as its lampposts and post boxes. So while Valys may not be as broad or modern as New Rondir is, it is definitely more majestic.

Captain Keldaron did not remain with me at the hotel for very long. Once I had been given the key to my room by the hotel staff, he told me he needed to report to his superiors at the Royal Palace, which is apparently just around the corner from "The Grand Unicorn". After that, he planned to have dinner with his elderly mother, who he has not seen for many months. The captain, as it turns out, is the youngest of six siblings, and the only male still alive (his two elder brothers perished in the most recent war with Troluska, some twenty years ago, which took place well before I was even born!).

When I was shown to my hotel room, I was rather surprised to find a number of packages sitting atop the bed. Those boxes are still there, unopened. But thanks to the note that accompanied them, I know that they were sent here by Captain Keldaron, and that they contain several lavish dresses from the most exclusive department store in Valys. You see, tomorrow I have an all-important meeting with the Royal Council of Alfynlund (the council that will choose the new king or queen of Alfynlund), and the captain understandably wants me to make a good impression. All I need to do is simply choose the dress that I like best. But rather than spend time looking at pieces of ridiculously expensive material, I decided to come out here, onto the balcony, and enjoy the view as much as possible before nightfall. After all, I have seen expensive dresses before (Mrs Greyfield and her daughters always wear the latest fashions), but this is the first time I have been in the magnificent city of Valys. The dresses can wait till tomorrow.

Today I finally got a taste of what life as a royal might be like. After I awoke, I had a quick bath and I ate a light breakfast, then I set about choosing a dress from the ones that Captain Keldaron had provided for me (on behalf of the government, I presume). I had expected that this would be an easy task, but alas, it was anything but! The dresses were all like something out of a fairy tale, and no matter how wonderful one dress looked, the next one never failed to look even more so.

It will hardly come as a surprise to you, I'm sure, but as a result of my indecision, I completely lost track of the time, and before I knew it, Captain Keldaron was knocking at the door. The captain appeared rather concerned when he saw that I was not yet properly dressed, and he told me that I needed to get a move on. I was truly at the end of my rope by then, so in utter desperation, I asked the captain to choose a dress for me instead. He chose a lovely red one, inlaid with flowery, golden designs around the neckline and the hem. After I hurriedly put the dress on, along with white gloves and shoes, we rushed downstairs to the front of the hotel, where there was a carriage waiting for us. But before we went to the Royal Palace, we stopped at a high-end beauty salon, called "The Emporium of Elegance". There, my hair was gathered up into a high bun, which is the way the ladies of high society in Alfynlund like to wear their hair these days. But that was not all. I also had make-up applied to my face, for the very first time in my life! By the time the industrious staff of the emporium were done with me, I could hardly recognise my own face in the mirror.

If the hotel I was staying at had seemed luxuriant, the Royal Palace of Alfynlund was doubly so. No matter where you looked, there was some sort of decorative feature, be it colourful wall-hangings or complete suits of gleaming armour. And there were also dozens of finely dressed servants and armed guards in bright, traditional costumes. But all of this I was only able to appreciate on the way out. On the way in, Captain Keldaron practically dragged me by the arm all the way to the Great Meeting Hall (where the Royal Council awaited us), and everything seemed to me to be just one big colourful blur. At one point, as we were running up a small flight of stairs, I lost a shoe. I tried to tell the captain about this terrible mishap, but he was so fixated on getting to the meeting hall on time that he completely ignored my cries of anguish. So I promptly decided to lose the other shoe as well. With the hem of my dress being so close to the ground, I reasoned that no-one would notice I was bare-footed.

The Great Meeting Hall was obviously designed with large gatherings in mind, for it had a very large rectangular table in the middle, one which could sit perhaps thirty or forty people at once. However, the council, which of course consisted of only a handful of people, had elected to gather in a corner at the far side of the hall. There, they were all sitting on a number of chairs that had been arranged more or less into a semi-circle. This left the greater part of the meeting hall conspicuously empty, and as Captain Keldaron led me across it, the captain's military boots echoed loudly throughout it. In contrast, my feet hardly made a noise. I think the captain noticed something was amiss, for at one point he glanced back at me with a puzzled look on his face, but he said nothing. In any case, we were soon standing right in front of the council.

Captain Keldaron introduced me by name, and briefly explained my situation and background. While the captain spoke, he had the council's complete attention, so I took the opportunity to discreetly study the men and women before me. Nearly all of them were elderly folk, with grey or white hair worn long, and nearly all of them were dressed in stylish green gowns. Two of the councillors, however, stood out from the rest. The first of these was the prime minister, who I recognised from the newspapers. Whilst his hair was quite grey, it had been cropped short and he was dressed in a formal suit. The other conspicuous councillor was not someone I recognised, but Captain Keldaron informed me afterwards that his name was Lord Delmyr, the newly appointed head of the Royal Church of Alfynlund. Apparently, his predecessor (the hundred-and-one-year-old fellow), had died suddenly just last week.

For someone in such a powerful position, Lord Delmyr looks incredibly young. At a guess, I would say that he is about the same age as, or perhaps, a little older than Captain Keldaron. He is tall, his hair is dark and long, and his face is pale and thin. He wore a gown of similar design to the ones that most of the other councillors had on, although his was pure white instead of green.

Once Captain Keldaron had finished speaking, the councillors all turned their attention to me, but no-one said anything. Instead, they all just sat there, staring. With so many cold eyes suddenly upon me (the coldest of which were the dark, penetrating eyes of Lord Delmyr), I began to feel rather uncomfortable. Eventually, however, Captain Keldaron asked one of the councillors (the Chief Keeper of the Histories of the Royal Family of

Alfynlund, or something like that) if he had anything he wanted to say. Pondering only for the briefest of moments, the white-haired individual declared that I looked too much like my Freelander mother and not enough like my Alfynlundic father to be the next ruler of Alfynlund.

I instantly felt my face flush red with anger. After having come halfway across the world because Alfynlund apparently needed my help, this was not the sort of greeting I was expecting. But before I could even think of what I should say in response to this rudeness, Lord Delmyr, to my utter shock, curtly rebuked his elderly companion, and the white-haired man apologised to me immediately. Needless to say, I was grateful to Lord Delmyr for his intervention, and to express my gratitude, I offered him a smile, but he merely continued to gaze at me, impassively. I found this rather unsettling.

In what I suppose was an effort to move on from this awkward moment, another councillor, one of the women this time, asked me why I had decided that I wanted to become a member of the Alfynlundic royal family in the first place. Well, if you've been reading this diary from the very beginning, you are no doubt aware that I don't really want to become a member at all. But of course, I couldn't just come out and say that. Luckily, Captain Keldaron had earlier suggested that if I was asked this particular question, I should say that I had an interest in learning more about my father's culture. It seemed like a rather flimsy reason to me, but most of the councillors seemed happy with this answer. Then came a series of questions of the sort that are often asked half-heartedly at social gatherings, such as what I thought about marriage and family. That was fine, but I was a little annoyed that during all this discourse, not one person present was kind enough to offer me a chair. But perhaps it was better that way. If I had sat down, everyone may have noticed that I was not wearing any shoes.

When the tedious questions finally dried up, there was another awkward moment, one where the councillors began wordlessly looking at one another, as if expecting somebody else to speak. In the end, Lord Delmyr announced that he thought I showed promise, but that the council would re-evaluate me after I had completed the intensive training course. Captain Keldaron was obviously pleased with Lord Delmyr's choice of words, and he told the council that he would send me to Nylanrod, where the intensive training course would take place, as soon as possible.

As Captain Keldaron and I made our way back to the front of the royal palace, I made sure to collect my shoes, both of which were thankfully right where I had left them earlier. Upon realising that I had been shoeless in the meeting hall, the captain was mortified. He exclaimed that if the councillors had noticed my bare feet, they would have thrown both of us out of the palace in an instant. I think he was exaggerating, but in any case, they hadn't noticed my feet, so what was the problem?

Tomorrow, I will be off to Nylanrod, which Captain Keldaron tells me is a three-hundred-year-old castle located in the southern mountains of Alfynlund. There, in a very short period of time, I will somehow be transformed into a true noblewoman. An impossible task if you ask me, but we shall see what happens.

As you can see, I did not write anything in my diary yesterday, the day I travelled from Valys to Nylanrod, where I am now. This is because yesterday was horrendously exhausting, and by evening I did not even have enough energy to pick up a pen. But today, I am feeling tremendously revitalised (due to the wonderfully fresh mountain air, no doubt), and so I am now able to relate to you yesterday's events.

After checking out of "The Grand Unicorn", I was required to visit several stores around Valys, where I collected a number of things that I would need for my stay in Nylanrod, such as books and practical outfits. That took most of the morning. At noon, precisely, I had lunch in a fancy restaurant. Once I was through eating, I went directly to Central Station (which conveniently lay within sight of the restaurant) and boarded a train bound for the southern town of Nelgrod. Then, from Nelgrod, a carriage took me along a winding dirt road, and through the woodlands at the foot of the mountains, to Castle Nylanrod.

This final leg of my journey was actually quite exciting. I had never seen any pictures of Castle Nylanrod and I was eager to see what it was like. However, the woodlands serve as a very effective screen, and you cannot see anything but trees and greenery until you reach the gate to the castle grounds. And that is where I saw it!

Castle Nylanrod is incredibly large, and with its many tall towers, it made me think of a giant white hand eagerly reaching skywards (albeit a hand with eight fingers). It stands directly behind the gate to the grounds, but to reach it, you must follow a road that circles around the edge of a small lake (named Lake Nylanrod, naturally). I thought that this was rather inconvenient at first, but when I saw Castle Nylanrod reflected in the mirror-like surface of the lake, I could almost believe that I had been magically transported to a place where castles float like clouds in the sky. It was truly an amazing sight, and for a brief moment, it seemed to me that becoming a royal might not be such a bad thing after all. But I soon remembered the reason that I had come here, and it was not to have a respite. Castle Nylanrod has been, for many years now, a school. But not just any school. It is a very special school, where young noblewomen study to become young noblewomen. I apologise if I seem a little flippant, but that is exactly how Captain Keldaron described Nylanrod to me yesterday. Being a soldier, I guess that etiquette is not something that he finds particularly interesting.

The headmistress of Nylanrod is one Grand Dame Parynfol, and it was she who was waiting for me at the main entrance to the castle. Contrary to my expectations, she is a delightful old lady, who wears magnificent, round eyeglasses (and who, incidentally, has equally magnificent eyebrows). She took me on a leisurely tour of the interior of Castle Nylanrod, showing me the sleeping quarters, the dining hall, the library and literally dozens of other places! Incidentally, we came across the class I'll become a part of gathered in one of the dance halls. There, the girls were all moving about most gracefully, like little birds in early spring. and the mere sight of this caused my heart to sink a little. Despite my slim build, dancing is something that, sadly, my body is not suited to.

It is now evening, and I'm alone in my private room, waiting to be called for dinner. I haven't quite finished unpacking my belongings, but I did unpack possibly the most important thing I brought with me from Valys, and that is the school uniform. Grand Dame Parynfol told me that I needn't worry about wearing it today, but I dearly wanted to put it on as soon as possible. It is rather quite pretty! It is mainly white, but it has a bright blue bow at the front and a pattern of thin vertical stripes, which are also blue. All the girls at Nylanrod wear it.

My room does not, unfortunately, have a view of the lake, but it does have a clear view of an imposing mountain peak that lies roughly eastwards of the castle. It is strange to think that somewhere on the other side of that mountain, and not a terribly long distance away, lies the border with the Kingdom of Troluska, which, if you are to believe what some of the newspapers in Valys are saying, is busily preparing for war with Alfynlund.

I have been very busy these past few weeks, far too busy, I'm afraid, to update my diary. This is hardly surprising, of course, if you consider that I am here at Nylanrod doing an intensive training course, but I never imagined just how incredibly busy I would be! Sometimes I feel as though I hardly have the time to even draw a breath. Today, however, was different. Today was a splendid late spring day, full of warm sunshine and wonderful scents, so Grand Dame Parynfol let us have a picnic by the lake instead of the usual classes. Therefore, as I sit here by the lake (upon which, incidentally, several waterfowl frolic), I will attempt to illuminate you on my life in idyllic Castle Nylanrod.

A typical day for me here involves attending classes for such things as etiquette, history and deportment. These classes start promptly after breakfast and end before dinner, with a short break at noon for lunch. After dinner, all the students are more or less free to do whatever they want to do. But not me, unfortunately. I have to spend my evenings studying Old Alfynlundic, because it is the language any future ruler of Alfynlund is expected to know perfectly. I find this class to be by far the most difficult, as by evening I am usually quite tired, and on more than one occasion I have dozed off in the middle of it. On a brighter note, I have successfully managed to avoid the dancing classes. This is because Nylanrod offers its students a choice between dancing or painting, and naturally I chose painting. I cannot in all honesty say my talent for painting is any better than my talent for dancing, but at least it is something I can do sitting down. And our teacher occasionally lets us go and paint outdoors, which allows me to not only admire the wonderful scenery of the castle grounds, it also allows me to spend some quiet time alone.

On reflection, when I first arrived in Alfynlund, I was sure that I would only do the bare minimum that was required of me. Now, however, I find myself strangely engaged in my activities. I guess part of the reason for this is that I never had a chance to attend a proper school when I was little, and so this is an interesting new experience for me. But the main reason is without a doubt Captain Keldaron. I remain of the opinion that I will never be chosen as the new ruler of Alfynlund, but even so, if I do not take my studies at Nylanrod seriously enough, the captain's reputation might possibly be tarnished, and I do not want that to happen. After all, it is thanks to him that my aunt is being well taken care of back in the Freelands.

Speaking of Captain Keldaron, he often comes to Nylanrod. This is, of course, mainly to discuss my progress with Grand Dame Parynfol. But he always takes the time to speak to me and offer me encouragement while he is here, and just last week he even brought me a letter from Aunt Tilu. You see, before I left New Rondir, the captain was thoughtful enough to make an arrangement with the Alfynlundic embassy there that would allow my aunt and I to write to one another. And although my aunt's letter made me feel a little homesick, it also lifted my spirits up tremendously. In turn, I hope that the letter I wrote in response will cheer up Aunt Tilu a little too, even though she hardly appears to be in any need of cheering up at all nowadays! Her health, Aunt Tilu tells me, has improved a great deal, so much so that she believes that there is a good chance she will be discharged soon. I hope my aunt doesn't rush things, but if she truly thinks she is feeling well enough, she'll be able to return to our little apartment, which, as you may recall, I paid several months of rent for, in advance.

On a more sombre note, the threat of war in the Oldlands has not abated. According to the latest rumours, there has been a steady build-up of soldiers on both sides of the border between Alfynlund and Troluska in the north, right where a major Alfynlundic industrial area lies. Here, at the foot of the southern mountains, we are well away from this potential flashpoint, but even so, hearing reports of this kind does nothing but amplify my stress.

I have just been informed by Grand Dame Parynfol that I'll be returning to Valys in a few days' time. But only for a little while. Apparently, the Royal Council wants to meet me again, so that they can evaluate how well I am doing in my studies. I'm not sure why this is necessary, however. The last time I spoke to Captain Keldaron, he mentioned that the council seemed to be favouring two other candidates, both of whom are Alfynlundic males, and that I was, at best, fifth choice on their list.

Of course, the idea of taking a little break from my studies in Nylanrod for a day or two is quite appealing, but I would honestly rather take a dozen dance classes than meet those dreary councillors again. And that goes double for Lord Delmyr. You see, during my time here in Nylanrod, I have learned quite a lot about a great many things, and I'm not just referring to my studies. Many of my fellow students are from prominent Alfynlundic families, which means they have access to news and information that the average person does not. And what they have told me about Lord Delmyr does not paint a pretty picture of him.

Lord Delmyr is quite an enigmatic individual, and much of his life before he became the head of the church of Alfynlund is a mystery. Indeed, the only thing that is at all clear is that he is the last surviving member of an extremely wealthy and influential Alfynlundic family, whose history goes back to the very founding of Alfynlund itself. He is often described as aloof and wily, if not downright cold and calculating, attributes that have obviously helped him rise to one of the highest posts in the land. But his sudden rise alarms many people, who say that he is much too young to lead the church, especially during these difficult times. And then there are those who go as far as to claim that he must have attained his position by using less than honourable methods, although nothing has been proven so far.

Despite his youth, however, Lord Delmyr is a staunch traditionalist, so it is no surprise that it is he who is behind the recent push to revive many of Alfynlund's ancient traditions. This includes, of course, the ceremony that the eventual successor to the crown of Alfynlund will have to perform in two months' time. Up until recently, I did not know a great deal about this ceremony, but I have been able to learn a little bit of what it involves from Grand Dame Parynfol. Basically, on the night of the summer solstice, a high-ranking representative of the royal family goes to the grandest church in Alfynlund, the "Temple of the Mother Tree", and performs a ceremonial dance whilst wearing traditional Alfynlundic attire. Following this, the representative recites an ancient incantation, which is basically a prayer to the "Mother Tree", beseeching her to continue to protect the elven people.

When I asked Grand Dame Parynfol about the origins of the ceremony (which is commonly referred to as the "Renewal Ceremony"), she told me that it began as a commemoration of a great tragedy that befell Valys many centuries ago. She then explained that when Valys was little more than a settlement (nearly two thousand years ago!), a great fire swept through it, killing half the population. The only reason more people didn't die was because many of them took shelter on Taloryl, a small island in the middle of the Iralas River, where a single but magnificent large oak tree stood. This tree would later become known as the "Mother Tree", and the famous "Temple of the Mother Tree" was erected around it.

Grand Dame Parynfol recalls travelling to Valys to watch the "Renewal Ceremony" on several occasions during her youth. However, the last time it was performed was many, many years ago, so she anticipates that this year's ceremony will attract a huge crowd of onlookers. Thank goodness, then, that in all probability I won't be the one who has to perform it!

Now I really must go to bed, as I need to be on the very first train to Valys tomorrow.

My second meeting with the Royal Council was not too dissimilar to the first. It took place in the same hall, with all the same people. However, there were two key differences. Firstly, nobody was dressed formally (except for Captain Keldaron and Lord Delmyr), and secondly, it was over in an instant. I was asked to introduce myself in Old Alfynlundic, which I did (rather poorly, no doubt), and then I was asked to perform a few dance steps. When I said I did not know any dance steps, there was a long moment of ghastly silence. The councillors then shared a few murmured words amongst themselves, after which I was promptly dismissed.

As I followed Captain Keldaron out of the Royal Palace, I was feeling awfully confused. The council had obviously been displeased with my responses. Did this mean they would be sending me back to the Freelands? I was just about to ask the captain this very question when someone called out to us from behind. It was Lord Delmyr! During the meeting, I'm sure Lord Delmyr had had the sourest expression of all the councillors, so it was quite a shock to see him approaching Captain Keldaron and I.

Lord Delmyr asked me when I would be returning to Nylanrod. I was unsure, so I looked to Captain Keldaron, and he informed Lord Delmyr that the plan had been for me to return tomorrow, but since the meeting had finished early, he thought it best for me to return on the noon train. Lord Delmyr then suggested that instead of leaving Valys straight away, I should visit the "Temple of the Mother Tree", where he would gladly give me a "private tour". I did not want to spend any more time with Lord Delmyr than was absolutely necessary, so naturally I thought this was a terrible idea. Unfortunately for me, though, Captain Keldaron thought it was a wonderful idea, and so I had little choice but to go with Lord Delmyr.

In spite of my reservations, I must confess that in the end my visit to the "Temple of the Mother Tree" was an interesting one. I got to see quite a lot of the temple, from its tallest spires to its deepest catacombs, and just about everything in between. I won't go into too much detail about the many things I saw, as there were simply too many of them, so I will only describe the thing that impressed me the most, which was the temple's central courtyard.

Despite being the very heart of the "Temple of the Mother Tree", the central courtyard is not very large. It is slightly rectangular in shape, and it is surrounded on all four sides by open corridors, which are stacked three levels high. Within the courtyard itself, there is a perfect carpet of lush, green grass, and a solitary oak tree. The tree is quite old and terribly gnarled, but at the same time very tall and strong-looking, with its broad branches (fully laden with leaves at this time of year) reaching nearly as far as the surrounding corridors. Yes, as you have probably already guessed, this tree is none other than the legendary "Mother Tree".

Lord Delmyr had not said a great deal up to this point of my "private tour", but as we were circling around the "Mother Tree", he suddenly asked me if I was excited about performing the "Renewal Ceremony". I found this to be a rather strange question, and I told Lord Delmyr that I thought it highly unlikely that the task of performing the ceremony would ever fall to me. For a very brief moment, a mere trace of a smirk appeared on Lord Delmyr's face, and he told me not to underestimate my chances, especially since I was a girl. When I asked Lord Delmyr what he meant by this, he looked genuinely surprised, and he asked me if I was aware of the special meaning behind the ceremony.

Not wishing to appear ignorant, I proceeded to relate, briefly, what I had learned about the "Renewal Ceremony" from Grand Dame Parynfol. Lord Delmyr looked dismayed, saying that I had simply learned the layperson's version of the ceremony. It occurred to me that Grand Dame Parynfol would probably not appreciate being labelled a layperson, but before I could say anything about that, Lord Delmyr began to tell me an alternative story about the origin of the "Renewal Ceremony", which was called "The Maiden and the Fire Giant".

Nearly two thousand years ago, when evil beasts such as dragons and giants still supposedly roamed the Oldlands freely, a particularly nasty tribe of fire giants emerged from the south. These brutes proceeded to ravage a large part of the region that would come to be known later as Alfynlund, attacking any elven tribes they found in their path.

Realising that something drastic needed to be done in order to stop the giants, the elven tribes came together and combined their forces, and this united elven army confronted the fire giants near the Iralas River. The battle that ensued was a terrible one. The elves succeeded in felling many of the giants, but at a terrible cost. Finally, battle-weary and with dwindling numbers, the elven army retreated into the river, in an attempt to get to the small island of Taloryl, where the elven women and children had taken shelter. The remaining giants, still in a state of battle-lust, foolishly pursued the elves into the river. Almost all of them drowned. However, one giant, the largest and most ferocious of them all, managed to reach the island, and he pursued the fleeing elven soldiers all the way to the elven camp, which stood near a large oak tree.

Seeing the approach of the monstrous giant, all the elves in the camp panicked, and they scattered like leaves before a gale. All but one young maiden, that is, who stood calmly beside the oak tree. The giant went straight for this brave girl, chasing her around the oak tree several times while simultaneouslys flinging fireballs in her direction. But the giant was neither able to catch the girl, nor strike her with its fireballs, and eventually it grew weary and fell to its knees. At this point, the girl offered up a prayer to the heavens, so that the elven people might be saved. Miraculously, her prayer was answered. The roots of the oak tree sprung out of the ground and wrapped themselves around the giant, like massive chains of iron. Try as he might, the giant could not break these roots, nor could his flames burn them, and they pulled him into the ground until he disappeared completely.

And so the elves were saved. Sadly, however, the brave young maiden (who by the way was named Valys) had over-exerted herself, and her life-force was all but spent. But before she died, the maiden warned her fellow elves that the giant's bonds were not permanent, and that they would need to be renewed at least once every generation.

"The Maiden and the Fire Giant" is an enthralling fairy tale, I'm sure you'll agree. But that's all it is, a mere fairy tale, regardless of how earnest Lord Delmyr's retelling of it may have been. And yet the thought of a massive monster, lying buried somewhere beneath the ground where I was standing earlier today, makes me feel uneasy, for some reason. But perhaps this is because I was the kind of child who is easily frightened by silly ghost stories. In any case, even if there really had been a giant, surely it would have died by now. I don't think even a giant could live for close to two thousand years, could it?

When Lord Delmyr declared that my "private tour" of the temple was over, it was already too late for me to catch the noon train to Nelgrod. (There is, incidentally, an evening train which I could have caught, but that arrives well after dark, and Captain Keldaron decided there was no need for me to get back to Nylanrod in a hurry.) So right now I find myself back in a familiar place, "The Grand Unicorn". This time, however, I am in a different room (one that is much smaller), and by some eerie coincidence, on the wall here there is an old painting titled a "Mighty Giant", which depicts a fire giant attacking a small elven village.

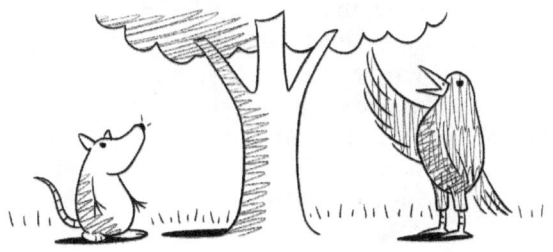

Today I find myself wishing that I had caught the late train back to Nelgrod yesterday. You see, when Captain Keldaron came to "The Grand Unicorn" this morning, he told me that there had been a change of plans and that I would not be returning to Nylanrod. Instead, I would be staying in Valys until the heir to the crown of Alfynlund had been chosen by the Royal Council. This was because Lord Delmyr had apparently decided that I was doing nothing but wasting my time in Nylanrod, and that, starting from tomorrow, I should instead begin practising for the "Renewal Ceremony" in the "Temple of the Mother Tree". I was unhappy to hear this, and not solely because the thought of being in close proximity to Lord Delmyr bothered me. I was also unhappy because I would now probably never get an opportunity to say "farewell", and "thank you", to Grand Dame Parynfol and the girls at Castle Nylanrod in person.

I guess my unhappiness was all too evident in my face because Captain Keldaron asked me if something was wrong. Not wishing to address my feelings towards Lord Delmyr directly, I simply stated that I thought Lord Delmyr's request was rather strange. Prompted to elaborate, I reminded the captain that there were, according to what he himself had told me not so long ago, several much more suitable candidates ahead of me. To my utter surprise, Captain Keldaron said that this was no longer the case. He then proceeded to inform me of news he had (incorrectly) assumed Lord Delmyr had imparted to me yesterday.

Apparently, the two leading candidates for the crown of Alfynlund (the two Alfynlundic males) were now no longer viable choices, as both had suffered serious mishaps in the last couple of days. One of them had taken a bad fall during riding lessons, and the other had become deathly ill after eating some rotten food by mistake. I was stunned by this news. It seemed too much of a coincidence that two of my "rivals" had both met with such unfortunate accidents at almost exactly the same time. It was almost as if someone was trying to make sure that I would end up being chosen as the next ruler of Alfynlund. But in any case, those two gentlemen weren't the only other candidates for the crown. There were at least two more. When I mentioned this to Captain Keldaron, he looked a bit uneasy. He then explained to me that another male candidate had suddenly gone missing about two weeks ago, and that two other female candidates had both recently decided that they were no longer interested in becoming royalty. When I asked Captain Keldaron how many candidates this left, he said just one. In other words, just me.

As I'm sure you can imagine, this was quite a bit of a shock to me. In a flash, I came to the frightening realisation that I will not be going back to the Freelands in a few months, as I had firmly believed I would. I honestly felt like screaming. What if, I asked Captain Keldaron rather angrily, I also no longer wished to become royalty, like those other girls? I had, after all, fulfilled my part of the deal. Had I not promised that I would stay in Alfynlund until I had completed the intensive training course? Well, thanks to Lord Delmyr's intervention today, the course was now over. The captain agreed that this was true, but he begged me not to be rash, suggesting that I wait at least until the eve of the Royal Council's decision. The candidate that has gone missing is being thoroughly searched for by the army, so there is a possibility, however slight, that he could be found before the decision is made. And as for the other girls, Captain Keldaron would speak to them himself in the hope of convincing them to reconsider. I seriously doubt that this will bear any fruit, but seeing how earnest the captain was did help me to calm down somewhat, and I told him that I would follow his advice.

And so this afternoon I moved from one fancy hotel to another. "The Phoenix" is less than a block away from "The Grand Unicorn", but it is a bit closer to the "Temple of the Mother Tree". I most certainly would not have minded having to walk an extra half block whenever I needed to go to the temple, but I guess that that is not the nobility's way of doing things. I do admit, however, that this new hotel has a much better view of the main thoroughfare in Valys. Dear me, what am I thinking? I certainly hope that this isn't a sign that I'm starting to get used to this high-class lifestyle, because it definitely won't last much longer. Despite all of today's developments, I still think it highly improbable that someone like me, a simple housemaid from the Freelands, will end up becoming the Queen of Alfynlund.

I had feared today was going to bring a whole heap of hardship with it, but in the end it was a mostly uneventful day. After breakfast, the first thing I did was go to the temple (as per Captain Keldaron's instructions), where a young servant quickly escorted me to Lord Delmyr's office. And when I say office, you probably imagine a small room with a desk and some other bits of furniture in it, but no, Lord Delmyr's office is nothing like that. It is huge! However, much of the floorspace is taken up with bookshelves, giving it the appearance of a well-stocked bookshop.

Lord Delmyr was at his desk, which sits at the far end of his office right, beneath one of many towering windows, busily writing a letter. A servant stood near him, completely still. He was so still, in fact, that I had to look at him carefully to make sure he was a real person, and not just a wax statue!

Lord Delmyr seemed not to notice my presence, so for a moment I was unsure of what to do, but thankfully the servant who had brought me to the office motioned to one of the many chairs nearby on his way out. It was only after I had sat down that I realised that I was not the only visitor Lord Delmyr had. Two other people had taken a seat. One was a tall and somewhat stern looking middle-aged lady, and the other was a diminutive old gentleman. The woman gave me a brief nod, whilst the old man gave me a big, friendly grin.

What seemed like an agonisingly long period of time

then passed, with the only sound being that of Lord Delmyr's pen scratching almost frantically on parchment, and this sound echoed eerily throughout the vast spaciousness of the office. When Lord Delmyr finally finished his letter, he folded it neatly and placed his seal upon it, then he held it up so that the servant near him could see it. Lord Delmyr did not speak to the servant, did not even look at him, but the servant at once took the letter from Lord Delmyr's hand and quickly exited the room.

Without any form of greeting, Lord Delmyr then began to explain to me what my daily schedule would be like, from now, until the Royal Council made its final decision. In the morning, I would take language lessons from Mrs Lyganol. In the afternoon, after a light lunch, I would take dance lessons from Mr Rolinuto. And then, after another short break, I would continue with the dance lessons in the evening. Mrs Lyganol and Mr Rolinuto were, of course, the other two visitors in the office, and they proceeded to politely introduce themselves to me.

Despite her apparent love of fine jewellery, Mrs Lyganol is a learned historian, who has published several books on the history of the Oldlands. She hardly smiles at all, but she does seem to know some interesting facts about many things, including things about the Freelands, which I had never heard of. But her task will not be to teach me trivia. It will be to make sure that I am able to recite the text for the "Renewal Ceremony" (which is entirely in Old Alfynlundic) flawlessly. If I don't, the invisible beings who repair the seal might not understand what I am saying and therefore won't do their job properly. If that happens, the fire giant will get angry and escape and eat everybody. Including me, probably. Or something like that.

Mr Rolinuto, a native of Gomonia, came to Alfynlund as a young man to pursue a career as a dancer (the art of dancing is held in much higher regard here in Alfynlund than in Gomonia). At the height of his career (which was many, many years ago), Mr Rolinuto was apparently quite famous, not only in Alfynlund, but the whole of the Oldlands. Now, however, he is retired and has to use a cane to get around. But despite this, he is an extremely cheerful person! So even though I detest dancing, I have the feeling Mr Rolinuto's lessons will at the very least be tolerable.

Once Mrs Lyganol and Mr Rolinuto had finished speaking, Lord Delmyr abruptly dismissed me, telling me I had the rest of the day to myself. It was a pleasant surprise, I must say, but once I had left the temple, I couldn't think of anything I really wanted to do. I have gotten so used to the repetitive nature of life in Nylanrod, that it feels strange to have to decide to do something on my own. It occurred to me to visit Captain Keldaron, but I knew he would be too busy to see me. In the end I simply wandered about the city streets, enjoying the scenery, until I got tired. Then I went back to my hotel room in "The Phoenix", where I found a package waiting for me. Inside the package was a simple dancer's outfit. It is a lovely, delicate thing, but it is a stark reminder that from tomorrow, I am going to be busier than ever.

I am sorry for neglecting my diary for so long yet again, but these past three weeks at the "Temple of the Mother Tree" have been so frightfully arduous. Far more arduous, in fact, than the time I spent at Nylanrod, which by comparison now seems like it was nothing more than a child's game. Having said that, though, a funny thing has occurred over the course of these past few weeks. At first I was very much convinced that the lessons at the temple would end up being a complete waste of time, but I have since changed my mind. And by that I don't mean that I have changed my mind about my chance of joining the Alfynlundic royal family. No, I simply mean that I have come to the conclusion that these lessons may one day prove useful.

Mrs Lyganol is as strict as my initial impression of her suggested, but even so, she does offer me encouragement when I need it, and on more than one occasion, she has even praised my earnest efforts. As for Mr Rolinuto, he is such a wonderful person! He does not chastise me at all when I make mistakes (and I tend to make a lot of them). On top of that, despite his frailty, he is ever so keen to demonstrate to me what it is I need to do. This actually serves as a great source of motivation for me. You see, I am terrified that in his overenthusiasm, poor Mr Rolinuto might fall over and hurt himself, so I'm doing my utmost best to get the dance moves right as quickly as I can.

I imagine that, judging solely by what I have written so far in this entry, I am giving the impression that all in all

I am coping quite well with the activities at the "Temple of the Mother Tree", despite their demanding nature. And that would be true to some degree, if not for one important factor. And that factor is of course Lord Delmyr.

When I first met Lord Delmyr, I think I was for the most part indifferent to him, but now I can honestly say that I dislike him, and this dislike grows stronger day by day. Every single day these past three weeks, without any sort of warning, he has come to check on my progress. And not just once or twice, but several times! Most times he says nothing, but when he does say something, it's never a compliment, only a rude remark.

During one of my very first lessons with Mr Rolinuto, Lord Delmyr was especially rude. After barely having had time to practise the dance steps for the "Renewal Ceremony", he had the nerve to say that I looked no better than a scarecrow caught in a tornado. Then he left. I was quite upset at this, but thanks to Mr Rolinuto's indefatigable cheerfulness, I soon forgot all about it.

And then there was the incident at today's lesson with Mrs Lyganol. Clearly unimpressed with my progress, Lord Delmyr made me recite the opening line of the ceremony over a dozen times, each time cutting me off midway and telling me to start over. Finally, he let out an exasperated groan and said, no, yelled at Mrs Lyganol that he could still plainly hear a trace of an accent in my pronunciation. Mrs Lyganol was left completely speechless by this, but I was not. I yelled back at Lord Delmyr, telling him that he was being quite unreasonable, as it is still anything but certain that I am the one who will be required to perform the "Renewal Ceremony". I was quite ready for Lord Delmyr to react angrily to this outburst, but, surprisingly, he kept quiet and simply looked at me in a curious manner. Then he stormed off.

Mrs Lyganol and I tried to continue the lesson, but she was clearly shaken by Lord Delmyr's reprimand. So after a while I told her that perhaps we should finish early today. She seemed relieved by this suggestion, but she did insist that we start a little bit earlier tomorrow, in order to make up lost time.

Lord Delmyr's criticisms aside, I am happy with my progress overall. If nothing else, the lessons have taught me that with a bit of effort, I can do things that, up until recently, I never dreamed I could do. Of course, I'm never going to become a world-class dancer like Mr Rolinuto or anything like that, but there may be a future for me as a dance or language teacher, once I return to the Freelands.

Caw! Caw!

May 13th, 1913 OC

I'm feeling awfully confused right now. Many things, unexpected things, happened today. First of all, not long after arriving at the temple for my earlier-than-usual lesson with Mrs Lyganol, I was swiftly intercepted by a servant, who told me that I needed to report to Lord Delmyr's office immediately. I had the feeling that I was going to get a dressing down for my behaviour yesterday (behaviour which, mind you, I do not regret in the slightest). But there was no dressing down. Instead, Lord Delmyr matter-of-factly informed me that Mr Rolinuto and Mrs Lyganol would no longer be my instructors.

Upon hearing this news, I felt like I had been struck by a thunderbolt. But as if this was not shocking enough, Lord Delmyr added that he will be my sole instructor from now on, so that he will be able to teach me the "proper" way to recite the text for the "Renewal Ceremony". And what about the dance which I have been working so hard to master for the past few weeks? Superfluous, according to Lord Delmyr. The only important thing is the text.

I was still in a bit of a foul mood from yesterday, so I wasted no time in complaining to Lord Delmyr that he was being utterly ridiculous to continue to put so much pressure on me, when the Royal Council was yet to make its decision regarding the crown of Alfynlund. That was when he unleashed another thunderbolt. He told me that he had called an emergency meeting of the council last night, and that they had decided, in the early hours of today, that I would be the one to fill the vacant throne of Alfynlund. By this point, I was starting to feel a little faint. But Lord Delmyr was not quite finished yet. He had one final thunderbolt left.

Lord Delmyr told me to return to my hotel room, and put on an outfit that he had ordered to be sent there a short time earlier. This was because the Royal Council would be making an official announcement on its decision at noon. Suddenly, terror gripped me. I had never been to such an event, let alone one where all eyes would undoubtedly be on me. As if reading my mind, Lord Delmyr told me that I needn't feel nervous about the announcement, as I would not be required to make any statement whatsoever, and that others, including Lord Delmyr himself, would speak on my behalf. However, this did little to calm my fear, and as I walked back to the hotel, my legs were literally shaking.

The outfit Lord Delmyr had spoken about was already waiting for me in my hotel room when I returned there, along with the person who had delivered it, and that person was none other than Captain Keldaron. Oh, what a great relief it was for me to see the captain. I had not seen him since I started studying at the temple. He also seemed pleased to see me, but there was an obvious look of concern in his face, and he asked if I was all right. I told him that I was most definitely not. Then I quickly explained to him what had transpired since the last time we had met, although it seemed he was already aware of the main points.

Captain Keldaron admitted that when he first heard that I had been the one chosen by the council, he did not believe it. And the reason for this was not that he thought of me as a terrible candidate, but that the choice had been made so suddenly and without the usual process.

According to his understanding, all remaining candidates were supposed to perform auditions for the ceremony, which would have helped the Royal Council choose the best overall candidate. But now, those auditions had been rendered pointless. I got the impression that Captain Keldaron suspected something was afoot, but he did not divulge that suspicion to me. Instead, he told me that I should steel myself for the whirlwind that was about to descend upon my life, beginning at noon today.

To be perfectly honest, I can hardly remember anything about the council's announcement. It took place on a small platform in the lobby of the same hotel I was staying at, and several extremely well-dressed officials spoke, including Lord Delmyr and the Prime Minister, but as Lord Delmyr had informed me, I did not need to say a single word. All I needed to do was merely stand in the background and smile. I did my best to do this, but my cheeks soon started to hurt. I did not realise how painful smiling could be on an occasion when you did not feel like smiling at all. As the speeches started to drag on, I began to feel dizzy once more, and it suddenly occurred to me that I had not eaten a thing since breakfast. The dizziness quickly worsened, and I think I was on the verge of fainting when somebody came up to my side. It was Captain Keldaron. He had come to offer his support (literally), so I leant on him to stop myself from suffering an extremely unceremonious tumble from the platform.

And so, thanks to the captain, I managed to survive this whole tedious affair. But even then, the torment did not stop, for once the Prime Minister had signalled the event was over, there was a surge of newspaper reporters towards the platform, all of them shouting out incomprehensible questions at me all at once. It was like standing in front of a pack of baying hunting dogs, barely restrained by their master's leash. And that was when I finally fainted.

When I awoke, I was back in my hotel room, lying on the bed. On one side of the bed stood Captain Keldaron. On the other was a man who I assumed was the hotel's doctor. The doctor smiled at me, then he looked at the captain and hold him that I would be fine after some rest.

Once the doctor left the room, Captain Keldaron sat down on the bed beside me. He fumbled with his hat for a long time with both hands before he said anything. Eventually, he told me he was sorry. When I asked him what he was apologising for, he at first simply said everything. But after a thoughtful pause, he went on to explain that if he had known just how difficult things were going to be for me in Alfynlund, he never would have been so insistent on bringing me here, all those months ago. I appreciated his words, but I told him that when I left the Freelands, I had more or less resigned myself to the possibility that this venture might take an unexpected turn, and that I am still willing to go through with it, if only for the sake of Aunt Tilu.

I'm not sure how much better my words made Captain Keldaron feel. All I know is that at the very least, they gave him some comfort, and therefore he felt able to leave me on my own for the remainder of the day. Now it is late in the evening, and having had a sumptuous dinner not so long ago, I myself feel much better than I did earlier today. And that is a good thing, because I am sure that tomorrow is going to be just as trying as today was, if not more so.

I am so tired. I hadn't realised that, apart from the announcement, there would be a number of other official engagements that I would have to attend. So, for the past two weeks or so, not only have I had to endure studying with Lord Delmyr, but I've also had to endure a great many tea parties and dinners.

As far as the lessons are concerned, they are more or less the same as the ones I had been having with Mrs Lyganol not so long ago. I am still learning Old Alfynlundic, albeit with a greater focus on the text of the "Renewal Ceremony". But Lord Delmyr, being as he is, somehow manages to make his lessons infinitely more tiresome. No matter how hard I try, my efforts never seem to satisfy him. And it certainly does not help one bit that Lord Delmyr is teaching me a different version of the text. When I asked why this was so, he explained to me that Mrs Lyganol had been using a slightly modernised version of the text. He much preferred the original version, and so that is what he is now teaching me.

As wearisome as Lord Delmyr's lessons may be, I find them infinitely more tolerable than the dreary parties I have been forced to attend lately. They all generally follow the same pattern. I arrive with great fanfare, then I am formally introduced to a great number of important people, such as imminent Alfynlundic citizens or delegates from foreign nations. I have even met with an official from the Freelands, who seemed thrilled with the idea of a Freelander becoming a regent. The thought crossed my mind to tell that official that if he liked this idea so much, I would more than gladly swap places with him. Of course, such a remark would only have created a moment of awkwardness, so I kept it to myself.

As exhausting as constantly meeting new people can be, that is not the worst part of these parties. You see, unlike the announcement event, I now have to make speeches. These speeches are all written for me by somebody else (most likely Lord Delmyr), so I guess I should be grateful for that at least, but I am expected to recite them entirely from memory, and given the little time I have to memorise them, I invariably make mistakes. This has obviously displeased Lord Delmyr greatly, but by now I've gotten accustomed to his constant complaining, and I just let it wash over me.

Thankfully, however, I've been told that the parties will all be done with in a few days. After that, the only thing I will have to do is put up with Lord Delmyr's lessons. And even those will not last very much longer, as the summer solstice will soon be upon us. Incidentally, I've heard absolutely nothing from Captain Keldaron in regard to the other remaining candidates for the crown of Alfynlund. So does that mean that, contrary to all my expectations, I will be the next ruler after all? I'm afraid to think about it too much.

Zzzzz...

Today, any lingering hopes that somehow someone else would be brought forward by the Royal Council as the next heir to the throne of Alfynlund have all but evaporated. And this is because today, instead of having my usual lessons with Lord Delmyr, I went to a place called "Lady Marydel's", the most famous dressmaker's shop in all Valys (or so I am told), to be fitted for my outfits for the coronation and the "Renewal Ceremony". The dress rehearsals for both of these events, you see, are now just days away.

As I'm sure you can imagine, the coronation dress will be something quite magnificent. It will be almost entirely dark blue, with gold embroidery on the bodice and lace at the collar, hem and sleeves. The other outfit, the one for the "Renewal Ceremony", is somewhat austere, but I guess the idea is that it supposed to be, to some degree at least, historically accurate. It will be made from a slightly coarse white cloth, with a number of patterns (such as the insignia of the temple of the "Mother Tree") woven into it with golden threads, and it will be sleeveless. The hem will be above my knees, but there will be several long cords hanging down from it, almost to my ankles. I imagine that when I spin around in this dress (and I will be performing a number of spins during the "Renewal Ceremony"), the cords will create a rather beautiful effect. The length of the cords concerns me a little, because they may cause me to trip, but I'm sure that any problems like this will be sorted out after the dress rehearsal.

The fitting took quite a while to get done, but even so it was still over before noon, so from "Lady Marydel's", I returned to my hotel room, where I had lunch. After I finished eating, I realised that I had the entire afternoon to myself for the first time in several weeks! The last time this was the case, I wandered about the city streets, but today the weather was inclement, so I decided to stay in the hotel. The trouble is, there's not a lot to do in a hotel room, even a luxurious one! There were a few newspapers lying about in the study, so I looked through those for a little while, but I soon grew tired of them. They were all full of reports of impending war. Funnily enough, I've been so busy of late, that I'd almost completely forgotten that Alfynlund is on the verge of war with Troluska. And so with nothing else left to do, I went to sit on a chair on the balcony (which is roofed).

As I watched the rain quietly falling on the streets of Valys, my thoughts turned to the Freelands, and in particular, to my aunt. Now that it is clear that I won't be returning to the Freelands any time soon, I realised just how much I missed her, and just how homesick I was. Then I started to cry. And cry. And cry. And cry. It was as if all of the stress that had built up inside of me over the past few months suddenly came pouring out like the water from a great big fountain. But I told myself that I could not simply spend the whole afternoon in tears. I had to find something to do. And the only thing that occurred to me at that moment was the thing that I had been doing ad nauseam for the past few weeks. That's right, I started to practise reciting the text for the "Renewal Ceremony". Funny, isn't it? And what's funnier is that, even though I've been working so hard to learn it for so long, I still don't fully understand what the text actually means. I did ask Mrs Lyganol one day to explain it to me, but she told

71

me that unfortunately we lacked the time to study the text in much detail. In the end, the only thing I gleaned from her was that the text is essentially a plea to the "Mother Tree", so that she will continue protecting the elven folk from the great evil that is still threatening it. The key line in the entire text is the final one, which is repeated three times, and which roughly translates to "bind to the Underworld". Interestingly, this line is the one that Lord Delmyr said Mrs Lyganol had taught me incorrectly. Instead of "bind" she was apparently teaching me to say "bear". I don't really see much difference in these two words, but then again, I am no scholar.

Reciting the text must have ended up calming me down much more than I thought it would, because at some point in the afternoon, I dozed off. When I awoke, which was not very long ago, night had well and truly fallen, and it was quite late, so even though I don't feel so tired now, I will be going to bed very soon.

June 19th, 1913 OC

Often I have wondered why I spend so much time practising for the "Renewal Ceremony", yet I do not spend any time at all practising for the coronation. Well, as I now know, the Royal Council had in fact decided many weeks ago that, in regard to the coronation, a single rehearsal would suffice, and it would therefore also be a dress rehearsal. What's more, this rehearsal had been scheduled for today! However, nobody remembered to tell me this important information. So you can imagine my shock when this morning, as I was preparing to go to the temple for my daily lessons with Lord Delmyr, one of the hotel's staff appeared at my door, and told me that there was a carriage waiting for me outside to take me to the Royal Palace.

Only when I arrived the Royal Palace did anybody bother to explain to me what was going on, and then I was immediately whisked away by palace staff to a small private chamber. There, I was helped into my coronation dress (the very one that I had been fitted for just a few days ago). By this point, I was starting to panic a little, as I was totally unprepared for a dress rehearsal. But of course there was nothing for me to do except go through with it.

From the chamber, I was taken to the throne room, where everybody who would be taking part in the coronation had gathered, such as Lord Delmyr and the prime minister. Even Captain Keldaron was present, looking very smart indeed in his navy-coloured dress uniform, but he was there in his capacity as a member of the royal guard. Therefore, he was with his colleagues the whole time, and I did not have a chance to speak with him at all. I have to admit that this saddened me, as it seemed to be a sign that in the future, I will be seeing a lot less of the captain.

To my tremendous relief, it turns out that the coronation is a simple affair, and this is basically what it involves. It all takes place in the throne room of the Royal Palace, and it begins with a speech from the prime minister, who will introduce me as the next ruler of Alfynlund. This is when I will make my grand entrance. I will join the prime minister in front of the throne, where I will stand until he is through speaking. After this, I will receive the blessing of the "Mother Tree", which will be administered by the head of the "Order of the Mother Tree" himself, Lord Delmyr, and during this ritual, all I need to do is quietly kneel in front of him. Only then will I be invited to take my place on the royal throne, where Lord Delmyr will place the crown of Alfynlund on my head, and I will make a solemn pledge to the people of Alfynlund.

Considering I had not been at all ready for today's dress rehearsal, I think I did quite well. But once it was over, Lord Delmyr and the prime minister immediately went over to talk to their fellow councillors, and left me sitting on the throne all by myself. This made me feel terribly annoyed. It was as if I was nothing more than a stage prop to them. So I decided to leave.

I had gotten about half a block from the Royal Palace when I heard a woman's voice calling out to me. The voice belonged to one of the palace staff who had helped me put on my coronation dress earlier, and she looked absolutely aghast. At that moment, I thought she was upset simply because I had carelessly exposed my beautiful coronation outfit to the elements, but thinking about it now, the real reason may have been the royal crown that was still sitting atop my head. In any case, she promptly led me back to the Royal Palace, where she and her fellow staff helped me change back into my much-less-formal-but-still-rather-formal clothes. After that, I returned to the hotel. And that was all that I needed to do today.

Tomorrow, the dress rehearsal for the "Renewal Ceremony" will be held, and I can't say I'm particularly looking forward to it. Unlike today's rehearsal, Lord Delmyr has stipulated that only he and I will participate, as in the end he is the one who has to determine whether my performance is acceptable or not. However, I'd prefer to have other people present. That way, the rehearsal won't end up being just another dreary private lesson with the cheerless Lord Delmyr, who seems to only want to speak to me when he has something to complain about.

Well, it seems that not even Lord Delmyr can get things his own way all of the time! Although he had been absolutely adamant that today's dress rehearsal for the "Renewal Ceremony" would involve only the two of us, this was ultimately not the case. Understandably, some of the other members of the Royal Council were still a little unhappy about Lord Delmyr unilaterally choosing me as the next ruler of Alfynlund, so he was forced to invite all of the councillors to the dress rehearsal, in an effort to reassure them.

The rehearsal was re-scheduled from early morning to midday, so that all the councillors would be able to attend it without much difficulty. This meant that I had to spend most of the morning alone in my hotel room, but this was to my benefit, as this gave me a chance to practise the dance that I have to perform at the very beginning of the ceremony. As you may recall, Lord Delmyr has only been instructing me in the spoken part of the ceremony, so I had not practised the dance element at all since Mr Rolinuto was dismissed. But once I started moving my body, the dance steps came back to me quite easily, which made me very happy.

Shortly before midday, I was taken to a small antechamber in "The Temple of the Mother Tree", where I changed into my outfit. As I have mentioned before, the outfit for the "Renewal Ceremony" is a very basic one, so I was able to change into it quickly and without any assistance (unlike yesterday's outfit). However, it did not come with any sort of footwear. Not knowing what else to do, I decided to keep my usual shoes on, even though their distinctly modern look clashes glaringly with the traditional look of the outfit. Soon afterwards, a servant arrived at the antechamber, and she took me to Lord Delmyr, who was waiting in front of his office. After looking me over very quickly, Lord Delmyr told me to take my shoes off and hand them to the servant. The "Renewal Ceremony", he said, was always performed in bare feet.

Lord Delmyr then led me down a number of corridors, and I soon realised that we were headed for the garden located at the rear of the temple, not the temple's courtyard, as I had expected. Perhaps noticing my confusion, Lord Delmyr explained that it is considered bad luck to recite the text of the "Renewal Ceremony" in the courtyard on any other day except the summer solstice, and therefore the rehearsal would be held in the garden. For me, this was not welcome news.

Even though it is now midsummer in Valys, there are occasional squalls that come in from the south, which bring a large amount of rain with them. Today, it had rained very heavily in the very early hours, and although it had stopped well before I left "The Phoenix", the ground in the gardens was sodden, and the wind was still quite strong. The other councillors were already waiting for us in the gardens, huddled together in a group. Almost all of them had coats or jackets on.

If it was up to me to grade my performance today, I would say that it didn't go particularly well. But that was entirely due to the extremely adverse conditions in the temple's garden. During the dance part of the ceremony, my feet quickly began sinking into the soil, and it was not long before they were completely covered in mud. Then, during the spoken part, the wind was so loud that I could hardly hear myself speak, so I seriously doubt any of the councillors heard me at all. Despite these problems, however, everyone present was apparently quite pleased, because after the ceremony was complete, everyone smiled and clapped politely. I guess with only a few days to go until the actual "Renewal Ceremony", they realised being critical would be counterproductive.

With the dress rehearsal over, and light rain starting to fall, we all hurried back to the temple. But when I saw that the temple's floors had been freshly waxed, I hesitated. All of the others had done an excellent job of avoiding getting more than a few small splotches of mud on their shoes. I, on the other hand, had mud caked onto my legs almost halfway up to my knees!

I immediately called for assistance, but just like after yesterday's rehearsal, the councillors were deeply absorbed in a discussion, and they soon abandoned me at the threshold of the temple's rear door. Although this was hardly unexpected, it was still terribly annoying. I was about to yell out something in anger, when suddenly, and seemingly out of nowhere, Captain Keldaron appeared. The captain at once offered to carry me to a room where I could wash my legs. As desperate as my predicament was, I found the idea of being carried rather silly, so the captain gallantly offered to lend me his boots instead. But this was an even sillier idea, so I reluctantly acquiesced to his initial offer.

On our way to the nearest bathroom, Captain Keldaron confided in me that he had watched my entire performance from an upstairs window, and that he had been impressed with it, especially since I had not had much time to practise. I think he was being overly generous with his praise, but I have to admit it greatly improved my mood and brought a smile to my face.

After I had washed my feet and changed out of my outfit (which will itself need a good wash), Captain Keldaron suggested I return to my hotel room immediately, so that I can have a proper rest for the coronation tomorrow. At first, I was not sure if this was a good idea, as I had the feeling Lord Delmyr would want to give me a critique of today's performance, but Captain Keldaron told me not to worry about Lord Delmyr, as he would deal with him.

Now, night has fallen, and I shall soon be going to bed, but I seriously doubt that I will be able to fall asleep easily. After all, tomorrow will quite possibly be the biggest day in all of my life, no matter how long I live.

I am now officially Queen of Alfynlund. And yet somehow I feel that this cannot be real, that this must be some kind of dream. But if it is a dream, it has not been an entirely pleasant one. There have been plenty of unpleasant moments in the last few months, the worst of which I experienced only a short time ago, at the coronation ball. But I will get to that later.

When I awoke this morning, I was still a "normal person", and so I set about doing "normal things". I got up. I ate something. No, in fact I didn't eat anything. I was too nervous to eat, and I simply stared at my breakfast for a while. Not long after, I was taken to the temple, where I got into my coronation dress (with a lot of help, of course), then I boarded an open carriage that took me to the Royal Palace. By that time, the sun was high in the sky and shining brightly, and a large number of people had lined the streets of Valys. Some people were holding flags and banners, and they cheered as I went past. Some people booed.

As numerous as the people on the streets had been, however, they were nothing compared to the masses who had gathered in the square before the Royal Palace. I can honestly say that that was the largest group of people I have ever seen. It was an overwhelming sight to say the least, so I was rather surprised to hear one of the councillors say to Lord Delmyr later in the day that she was disappointed that more people had not turned out. In response to this, Lord Delmyr said that some people were still not used to the idea of a monarch who was Half-Freelander, but he was confident that they would get used to it very soon.

I was particularly anxious during the ceremony itself, so I can hardly recall anything about it. All I know is that it seemed to go smoothly. Everything happened more or less in the way that it was supposed to, including the part where I pledged to do my best to protect and serve the people of Alfynlund for as long as I lived. And before I knew it, it was all over. Now that I think about it, the whole thing was not too dissimilar to getting married. The only difference was that instead of being bound to a person, I had been bound to a title.

With the conclusion of the coronation ceremony, the many dignitaries and guests began making their way to City Hall, where the coronation ball was to be held. Naturally, as the new ruler of Alfynlund, I also went to the ball, but not before changing into a lovely, pale yellow evening gown, which I am told was a gift from Gomonia.

I had thought that by this time, all the hard work had been done and all that was left for me to do was relax. But I had forgotten that I was now a member of high society. So before any eating, drinking or dancing took place, I spent what felt like hours being formally introduced to the rich and famous people of Alfynlund. I tried to be as polite as I could during this whole tedious process, but I wasn't really paying much attention to what was being said. And if I were to run into any of these people again tomorrow, I am certain I would not recall their name. Apart from one, that is. And that person was the incredibly tall and proud-looking ambassador from Troluska, Mrs Aralisnova. I had never met a Troluskan before, and all I knew about the Kingdom of Troluska itself was only what I had read in the newspapers, which painted a picture of an angry, violent group of people. But after speaking with the ambassador, I'm convinced that this is not true.

After I mentioned to Mrs Aralisnova that I had studied in Nylanrod, she invited me to visit the mountains in her country, saying that they are just as beautiful as the ones in southern Alfynlund. Of course, the way things are between Alfynlund and Troluska at the moment, it is highly unlikely that the Royal Council would allow me to go anywhere near Troluska, but I would certainly like to visit Mrs Aralisnova one day.

After the introductions were all done with, the dancing began. But since I had been standing up for such a long time, my feet were already quite sore. So, in order to get a bit of rest and some fresh air, I went to sit down on a chair by the doors to the balcony, both of which were wide open. Looking about the ballroom, I spotted Captain Keldaron. Unfortunately for me, however, he was still on guard duty, and therefore there was no chance of speaking with him, let alone dancing with him. Not that I had any desire to dance, mind you. As I have written in the past, I don't have much talent for dancing, but if for some reason I had been required to dance at least once during the ball, I would have wanted to dance with Captain Keldaron. However, all this is mere conjecture now, for what happened next effectively ended the ball, for me at least.

As I sat by the balcony, watching the multitude of couples twirling about on the floor in front of me, I heard a sound behind me. It was a loud groan, the kind people make when they are making great physical exertions. Looking over my shoulder, I was shocked to see a rather dishevelled old man, with glassy eyes and long, unkempt grey hair, climbing onto the balcony. There was too much noise in the hall at that moment for anybody but me to have noticed this intruder, and I immediately thought to raise the alarm. But before I could do anything of the sort, the old man began yelling. His speech was slurred, so what he was saying was not altogether clear, but he seemed to be speaking about the end of days, and that Alfynlund would soon be engulfed by a terrible calamity, one of its own making. As you can imagine, the music and the dancing all suddenly stopped, and the Royal Guards leapt into action. Very soon, the seemingly deranged old man was pinned to the floor by no less than six of the Royal Guards. One of these was Captain Keldaron, but seeing that his colleagues had the situation well in hand, he came to my side and asked if I had been harmed in any way. I told him I was fine.

The prime minister, who was hosting the ball, tried to make light of the situation, and he invited everyone to continue enjoying the evening. But when he came over to where I was, he was visibly concerned, and he told Captain Keldaron that I was to be taken back to the Royal Palace at once.

And that is how today, my first day as Queen of Alfynlund, ended. Now, I am lying in my enormous and luxurious bed in my enormous and luxurious private chamber in the Royal Palace, my new home. Out of all the places I have stayed at in Alfynlund, this would surely have to be the safest. But even so, the incident at the coronation ball has left me more than a little shaken.

My thoughts turn to dear Aunt Tilu. I put aside her most recent letter, unopened, with the intention of reading it when I would be able to do so at my leisure. However, due to my relocation to the Royal Palace, I have misplaced it. I feel terrible about this. I wonder what my aunt wrote in that letter. I hope it was good news. I hope she is feeling better. But I mustn't think too much about my aunt, just like I mustn't think too much about what happened this evening. And that's because I need to focus on tomorrow's "Renewal Ceremony". Hopefully, it will go well, and nothing bad will happen.

As I write this, my hands are shaking a little. I am here, at the "Temple of the Mother Tree", and very shortly, I will be performing the "Renewal Ceremony". But it is not because of stage fright that I'm feeling so nervous. You see, there's been a late change of plans. Unlike in the past, the ceremony will not be performed in front of the public, and you'd think that such a change would make me feel a lot better, wouldn't you? But that is not the case. And this is because of the reason behind the change. According to Lord Delmyr, there is genuine concern that during the ceremony an attempt may be made on my life.

I learned about this frightening new development not long ago, at an extraordinary emergency meeting of the Royal Council that took place at the Royal Palace. As both Queen of Alfynlund and the potential victim, I obviously attended this meeting. Captain Keldaron, as head of security for the "Renewal Ceremony", was also there. The meeting began with Lord Delmyr referring to the incident at the coronation ball, yesterday evening. He said that the old man who had broken into City Hall had been searched and questioned. A small knife was found concealed in his clothing, but his words remained largely incoherent, spouting forth such vague proclamations as "the end of the Mother Tree" and "the end of Alfynlund". For Lord Delmyr, however, this was proof enough that the old man had gone to City Hall with the intention of attacking me. Furthermore, there was no way of knowing whether the old man was working alone, or as part of a larger group. Which group he was referring to exactly was left unstated, but he seemed to be hinting at a foreign power (almost certainly Troluska).

After Lord Delmyr had finished speaking, two camps formed, and a heated discussion took place. On one side, there was Captain Keldaron's camp, who wanted the "Renewal Ceremony" called off entirely. On the other was the prime minister's, who wanted the ceremony to go ahead as planned, but with heightened security measures. (For the record, my preference was for cancelling the ceremony, but I was prepared to go through with it if it was deemed safe to do so.)

I'm positive that this discussion could have gone on for weeks, since both camps were adamant that their proposal was the better one, but in the end, Lord Delmyr offered a compromise which both camps could agree to (albeit reluctantly). The ceremony would go ahead, with increased security, but no public.

With that, the meeting ended, and Lord Delmyr ordered Captain Keldaron to take me to the "Temple of the Mother Tree" as soon as possible. So, not long after, the captain and I boarded a closed carriage and made the relatively short journey from the Royal Palace to the temple. Travelling with us was a large group of soldiers, but even so I don't think I've ever had a more nerve-wracking trip in all of my life, and the only thing that kept me calm was the fact that Captain Keldaron was with me.

After we arrived safely at the temple, I confided to Captain Keldaron that I was not entirely convinced that Lord Delmyr's assessment of the incident at City Hall was correct. If the old man had indeed meant to attack me, surely he would have taken out his weapon by the time he staggered into the ballroom. But I never saw it. Also, I mentioned to the captain that I did not think it possible that Troluska was behind all this. I may be young, but I believe that I am a good judge of character, and Mrs Aralisnova seemed to me to be a very decent person. If the people she represents are even half so, I do not think that they would desire a costly conflict with Alfynlund. In regard to all this, Captain Keldaron did not say whether he agreed with me or not. But he did agree with me when I remarked that there was little point in holding a ceremony if there was going to be next to no one to watch it.

So now here I am, sitting in a familiar little antechamber by myself. I am already dressed for the "Renewal Ceremony", and I am waiting for the squad of elite Royal Guards that will escort me to the courtyard. Lord Delmyr advised me that I should spend the time before the ceremony going over the text, but I think I've done that more than enough times already. Instead, I find myself thinking about the Valaryn Syldanor of old, the simple housemaid from the Freelands. My goodness, it seems like a lifetime since those days in New Rondir, when I worked at Greyfield Manor. Those were long, tiring days, but strangely enough, I find myself wanting to return to them, if that was somehow possible.

I can hear the sound of approaching boots. I assume that they belong to Captain Keldaron and his colleagues. I still feel quite nervous, but there is nothing I can do about that now. I am Queen of Alfynlund and I have to do what is expected of me, no matter what.

I'm writing this with a pencil and a piece of paper which a kindly nurse gave to me, just a few moments ago, but I will be sure to transcribe this into my diary after I leave hospital. Yes, I am in hospital right now. And since I have no idea when I will be discharged, I thought it prudent to write down last night's events before I start to forget any important details.

So what happened last night? Quite a lot, in fact. Unbelievable things. Terrible things. But despite all that happened, I'm still alive. And I'm grateful for that.

The ceremony started out innocuously enough. When I walked out into the courtyard, it was a cool but clear night, and the "Mother Tree" stood tall and dark against the starlit sky. The area immediately surrounding the tree had been carefully roped-off, in anticipation of a large crowd, but of course due to Lord Delmyr's directive earlier in the day, there was no crowd, only officials. Chief among these was Lord Delmyr, along with several of his acolytes, who stood in a circle around the "Mother Tree", just inside the rope. All of them were wearing the splendid ceremonial gown of the "Order of the Mother Tree", which is white with golden adornments. The only other people in the courtyard were the Royal Guards, led by Captain Keldaron, and they lined the perimeter of the courtyard, dressed in their ceremonial dress, which is, of course, navy-coloured.

I solemnly approached the "Mother Tree" (as Lord Delmyr had instructed me), and then I turned around so that I was standing with my back towards it. There I waited for the signal from Lord Delmyr to begin the first part of the ceremony, the dance. This was because the dance had been planned to coincide with a magnificent fireworks display (which symbolised a fire giant's fireballs). It seemed to take an awfully long time for Lord Delmyr to give me the signal, but when it finally came, I went straight into the dance around the "Mother Tree".

The fireworks were launched from the temple's garden, which is literally no more than a stone's throw away from the courtyard, so the noise they made was deafening, and the light they produced was blinding. The fireworks also produced a lot of smoke, which the wind blew right across the courtyard. Needless to say, these were things I had been completely unprepared for, and they were terribly distracting. I did manage to get through the dance in the end, but it was messy. I dread to think what dear Mr Rolinuto would have thought of it had he seen it.

After the end of the dance (and the accompanying fireworks display), I took a brief moment to catch my breath before starting the spoken part of the ceremony. I spoke as loudly as I could without screaming (again, as Lord Delmyr had instructed me), and my words echoed around the courtyard. When I uttered the last sentence (the one that is repeated three times), I realised something was not quite right. The acolytes near me suddenly started looking at each other rather nervously. Had I made an error? I turned to Lord Delmyr, and he was looking directly at me, smiling. Up to that point, I don't think I had ever seen him smile. But his smile was not at all a comforting sight. It was something quite sinister.

As I pondered the meaning behind Lord Delmyr's strange expression, one of the acolytes approached Lord Delmyr, with a worried look on his face. By then, I was sure that I had said something wrong. But how could that be? I had recited the words exactly as I had learned them from Mrs Lyganol! No, that was not true. Lord Delmyr had altered the text slightly. But why had that upset the acolytes? I felt very puzzled by all this, but before I could think upon it for too long, the ground beneath me began to shake.

Although I had never experienced one in all my life, I at once told myself that this was an earthquake, and since I was standing in the middle of an open courtyard, I felt reasonably safe. All I needed to do was wait for the shaking to stop. But the shaking got steadily worse, and soon, acolytes and guards alike were toppling over. Eventually, I fell down, too. Then, in the ground around the "Mother Tree", large, gaping cracks started appearing. These cracks quickly grew in size, and just when I thought one of them was going to swallow me up whole, the shaking suddenly stopped.

I clumsily got to my feet and I saw others around me doing the same. Out of the corner of my eye, I think I saw Captain Keldaron desperately hurrying towards me. I was about to call out to him, to let him know that I was all right, when an almighty roar, like that which a huge, enraged bear might make, rose up from somewhere beneath the ground. The entire courtyard seemed to bulge upwards in response to this guttural cry, and it continued to do so until the tension became too much. Then, the courtyard crumbled into a million pieces. After a brief sensation of falling through the air, I landed awkwardly in what seemed to be a large, dark pit, and I felt a sharp pain in the lower part of my back. Then everything went black.

When I came to, I found myself looking at the concerned face of Captain Keldaron. For a while, I wasn't sure at all what was what. Was I waking from a dream? Was I dreaming I was awake? But then I became aware of the pain in my back, and I realised that neither what had happened in the courtyard, nor what was happening now was a fantasy.

Looking around, I saw that I was lying on the ground in the temple's garden, where there was an incredible amount of activity going on. Hospital staff were tending to several injured people, most of who I recognised as the acolytes that had been standing near me during the ceremony. This was a distressing sight in itself, but there were also a few mounds amongst the injured, which had been roughly covered by blankets. There was no mistaking what these mounds were.

Once I had taken all of this in, I turned my attention back to Captain Keldaron, who was kneeling on the ground beside me, asking me how I was. I told him that apart from the pain in my back and a few scratches here and there, I seemed to be all right. Then I asked the captain to tell me how it was that I ended up here, in the garden. The captain explained that he himself had carried me out of the pit I fell into, a few moments ago. Despite the situation, I found myself filled with admiration for the captain. I know I don't weigh very much, but it certainly cannot have been easy for him to clamber out of that pit whilst holding me at the same time.

It suddenly occurred to me that Lord Delmyr was nowhere to be seen. When I remarked on this, Captain Keldaron informed me Lord Delmyr was missing, but there was a search underway for him. I was about to tell the captain of the strange way Lord Delmyr had been behaving the last time I saw him, when the ground started to shake once more. This shaking went on for quite a while, and it was followed by the loud sound of splintering wood and cracking stone. The entire northern side of the "Temple of the Mother Tree" was beginning to collapse.

The din of the falling rubble was enormous, but above it all, I clearly heard someone yell out. It was one of the Royal Guards, and he was frantically pointing towards the courtyard, which as a result of the cave-in, was becoming fully exposed to the garden. Smoke was rising from the ground in the vicinity of the "Mother Tree", but it was a peculiar kind of smoke. It had a slight orange tinge to it, as if there was a large fire burning beneath it. The next thing I knew, a giant, red-coloured hand emerged from the ground, and it was covered with thousands of little tongues of flames, which rippled like hair in the wind. It was quickly joined by a second hand, and then, with an ear-splitting roar, a giant head appeared, with what looked like a large bonfire atop its head. The giant slowly pulled itself out of the ground, and as it did so, the night was filled with such bright light, that you could almost think it was daytime once more. The giant looked towards where we were gathered, and then it took a slow, long stride towards us.

As you can imagine, panic instantly ensued in the makeshift field hospital, and doctors began yelling at everyone to move away from the advancing monstrosity as quickly as possible. Those who could walk did so, the rest were carried. Captain Keldaron tried to get me to stand, and only then did I realise that I could not move my legs at all. When I told the captain this, his face filled with concern once again, but without a word he picked me up and hurried away from the temple. Some people decided that the best course of action was to climb over the garden wall, even though that wall is well above the height of the average adult male. Everyone else decided to head for the nearest side gate. Captain Keldaron, being encumbered with me as he was, joined the latter group. When we got to the gate, however, it was chained shut. A temple servant made an awkward attempt to climb up and over the gate, but Captain Keldaron told him to get back down. He had a plan.

After setting me down on the grass, Captain Keldaron pulled out his revolver. The chain holding the gate shut was not very thick, but it still took the captain three shots to break it. With the gate opened, the people around me quickly streamed out of the temple grounds, heading southwards and away from the giant along an open field, in the direction of the nearest main road. Captain Keldaron put his weapon away and then came to collect me. But as he was about to step through the gate, I told him to stop so I could check on what the fire giant was doing.

At that moment, the monster had just about reached the people who had as yet been unable to clamber over the garden wall. It was painfully obvious that not all of those people would be able to escape with their lives. I suddenly felt incredibly guilty. I was certain that the catastrophe that was unfolding right before my eyes was the result of my failure, and tears began falling down my face. Captain Keldaron tried his best to console me, but I could not stop crying. I explained to the captain, as best as I could, that I must have recited the text incorrectly. And then it dawned on me. Yes, I had made a mistake, but only because Lord Delmyr had wanted me to make a mistake. He had taught me an incorrect version of the text on purpose, so that the "Mother Tree" would release its grip on the giant, not tighten it! What his aim in doing so was, I do not know, but I did know that there might be a way to correct my mistake. I told Captain Keldaron to take me back to the

"Mother Tree". The captain thought I was crazy, and that it was much too dangerous to return there, but I insisted, and in the end he relented.

As Captain Keldaron carefully carried me through the debris of what had once been the rear section of the "Temple of the Mother Tree", I explained my plan to him. If I recited the correct text, not the one that Lord Delmyr had taught me, I thought that perhaps the "Mother Tree" might be able to recapture the fire giant. Captain Keldaron admitted it was worth a try.

Upon reaching the "Mother Tree", the captain set me down close enough to it so that I was able to sit up against it, and then I quickly recited Mrs Lyganol's version of the text. The ground around us convulsed, much as it had during the ceremony, but it soon stopped. The giant, which was at that very instant crashing through the garden wall, was completely unaffected. I determined that the giant was now well beyond the reach of the "Mother Tree", and that therefore we needed to lure it back to the courtyard somehow. Captain Keldaron concurred, but he decided there was no need for both of us to risk our lives in doing this. With that, he started to move away, but he paused briefly to offer his revolver to me, so that I could protect myself during his absence. I responded by telling him that I did not know the first thing about guns, and therefore it would be of little use to me.

Once I was by myself, I reflected on all that had just happened. It was all so surreal! As far as I could tell, there was hardly anyone in Alfynlund who really believed the story about the origin of the "Mother Tree". And so I had not really believed it either. In fact, the only one who seemed to take it at all seriously was Lord Delmyr. But had he foreseen this disaster? Or rather had he planned for this disaster?

I was lost in thoughts such as these when I heard someone approaching. But it was not Captain Keldaron. It was Lord Delmyr. He was still dressed in the tunic he wore for the ceremony, although it was now covered almost completely in dirt. This suggested that he had fallen into the pits created during the earlier upheavals, like I had. However, unlike me, Lord Delmyr did not appear at all hurt, and he had the same unsettling expression he had had when I last saw him. I feared that he had gone mad, but when he spoke to me, his words were clear and eloquent. He thanked me for my contribution to his great plan, and that my name would without any doubt be permanently inscribed into the annals of the Kingdom of Alfynlund. Naturally, I had absolutely no idea what he was talking about, so I asked him to elaborate. Lord Delmyr gladly obliged.

For centuries, the Kingdom of Alfynlund had been a great and powerful land, but according to Lord Delmyr, it had largely lost its way in recent times. It had grown corrupt and decadent, and this wretched display of weakness was all but inviting an invasion from its traditional enemies, the chief of which was, of course, Troluska. If Troluska were to attack in force, Alfynlund, in its weakened state, would not be able to stand for very long. Therefore, before that sad eventuality, a spark was needed, one that would bring life back into Alfynlund, and restore it to its former glory. The giant from the tale of "The Maiden and the Fire Giant", the giant whose very existence had been forgotten by everyone except for a handful of true believers, was perfect for this.

In essence, Lord Delmyr's plan was quite simple. It involved releasing the giant, letting it run amok in Valys, and then letting the Alfynlundic army deal with it. Faced with the terrible destructiveness of modern weaponry,

Lord Delmyr did not think the giant would last until sunrise. Nevertheless, in that time it would cause such havoc that the long dormant fighting spirit of Alfynlund would reawaken once more. Yes, it was indeed in essence a simple plan. But there was one major obstacle it had to overcome. The giant could only be released by a member of the Royal Family (as only a royal had the right to perform the "Renewal Ceremony"). What's more, that particular individual had to somehow be convinced to recite the text incorrectly. And that is, of course, where I came in. As a commoner from a foreign land who understands next to nothing of the Old Alfynlundic tongue, Lord Delmyr determined that he would be able to manipulate me quite easily. And judging by the events unfolding in Valys at that very moment, Lord Delmyr was confident that he had determined correctly.

When Lord Delmyr had begun his overly long monologue, I had been frankly quite afraid of him. After all, he spoke of terrible things, such as death and calamity, in an unnaturally detached, matter-of-fact way. But the longer he spoke, the less afraid I became. And then, before I even realised I was doing it, I was angrily yelling at Lord Delmyr to be quiet. Lord Delmyr looked a little taken aback by my outburst, and he stopped talking. I must admit, after months of being ordered about like a trained animal, I found the act of letting out some steam oddly satisfying. Perhaps that is why, rather than leave it at that, I foolishly went on to tell Lord Delmyr that although he had tricked me into helping him fulfil his evil plan, it was too early for him to claim victory. There was still time for me to try to return the fire giant back to the depths of the ground from where it had escaped from. Lord Delmyr said nothing, but his face quickly drained of all emotion and became almost deathlike. Then he calmly pulled out a dagger from inside his robes and started advancing towards me.

I would have screamed at this point, but before I could even open my mouth to do so, a powerful roar suddenly shook the night, startling both Lord Delmyr and I. It was the giant! Evidently, Captain Keldaron had succeeded in drawing it back towards the courtyard, and it was now plodding its way back to the "Mother Tree".

Lord Delmyr was left stunned by this turn of event, so I took the opportunity to toss a clump of dirt at his knife, in the hope that I could dislodge it from his grip. Unfortunately, however, I only succeeded in hitting his knee, and as a consequence, I brought his attention straight back to me. A look of fury filled his face, and he told me I would not live long enough to do anything that could interfere with his plan. Then, gripping his weapon firmly, he took a step in my direction.

All of a sudden, there was a bang. Lord Delmyr gave a loud, pained gasp, before he promptly dropped his weapon and fell to the ground in a heap. Behind him, quite a distance away, stood Captain Keldaron, brandishing his revolver. I let out a huge sigh of relief.

Captain Keldaron came running to my side and asked if I was all right. But before I could respond, Lord Delmyr suddenly got back to his feet and leapt onto the captain. Both men tumbled to the ground, and in the ensuing struggle, Captain Keldaron dropped his gun. Lord Delmyr made a desperate grab for the weapon, but this only allowed Captain Keldaron to easily pin Lord Delmyr to the ground. Lord Delmyr writhed violently, like a savage animal, but the captain's grip held firm. Nevertheless, I was worried Lord Delmyr might break free at any moment, so I started to drag myself to the spot on the ground where the gun lay, but Captain Keldaron yelled at me not to bother, and he told me that I should concern myself with the giant instead.

I had momentarily forgotten about the giant, to be honest. By this time, it had crossed the perimeter of what had once been a picturesque courtyard, but which now resembled a heavily bombarded battlefield, and it was continuing its advance towards the "Mother Tree", perhaps drawn by the ruckus Lord Delmyr was making. Captain Keldaron, still holding Lord Delmyr down, told me to start reciting the text immediately, but I hesitated, thinking that the giant needed to be as close to the "Mother Tree" as possible. So I waited.

The giant's footsteps steadily became louder and louder, until the "Mother Tree" itself began to shake from the vibrations they caused. Again, Captain Keldaron told me to start reciting the text. But still I waited. I waited until I could feel the heat radiating from the giant's body on my face. Then, at last, I recited the words of the "Renewal Ceremony". The correct ones, this time.

The ruined surface of the courtyard convulsed yet again, but this time the massive roots of the "Mother Tree" shot up into the air, like the tentacles of the massive undersea creatures that sailors claim dwelt in the deepest of oceans. Several of the roots wrapped themselves around the legs of the giant. As a result, the giant's advance was slowed, but not stopped, so I recited the text for a second time. More roots appeared, and these grabbed the giant about its waist, finally bringing the monster to a halt. The giant let out a loud cry, as it strained against the grip of the roots, and some of the roots began to snap. So I recited the text a third time, and new roots replaced the broken ones, some of which grabbed the giant by the neck. The giant lost its balance, and it collapsed onto its back, with a thunderous crash that created a massive cloud of dust. For an instant, I was left blinded and barely able to breathe. But the dust was soon cleared away by the wind, and by the time I could see clearly again, the giant was nowhere to be seen. The ground had swallowed it up completely.

Faced with utter defeat, Lord Delmyr finally gave up struggling, and started wailing sorrowfully. This allowed Captain Keldaron to calmly unbuckle his belt, and with it he bound Lord Delmyr's hands together tightly. Then, after collecting both his firearm and Lord Delmyr's dagger, the captain came to my side. He didn't ask how I was, because he already knew I was hurt. He simply picked me up gently and said that we needed to get to a doctor as soon as possible.

As Captain Keldaron carried me out of the ruined courtyard and away from the damaged temple, I looked behind us, at Lord Delmyr. He was still lying on the ground, sobbing uncontrollably. And I also saw the "Mother Tree", standing as tall and as proudly as ever. My eyelids began to grow heavy at this point, but just before they closed completely, it seemed to me that the "Mother Tree" was no longer a tree, but a tall woman with long flowing hair that billowed upwards from her head in all directions. And that is the final thing I remember seeing last night, before I passed out from sheer exhaustion.

I awoke here today, around midday, in a large city hospital located only a short distance from the "Temple of the Mother Tree". I asked the doctor who examined me not so long ago if he thought I would be able to recover the use of my legs. He replied that it was not out of the question, but his grave expression told me that he was only saying that to make me feel better.

I desperately want to find out how Captain Keldaron is. I have not seen him since last night, but I trust that he is well. As for Lord Delmyr, I haven't heard anything about him, either. And, of course, I have no idea what effect last night's incident had on Alfynlund and its people. I do hope that somebody will be able to provide me with information about all of these matters sooner rather than later.

As you can see by the date above, a long time has passed since I last wrote anything in my diary. It is now early autumn, and I am back in my little apartment in New Rondir, sitting in my wheelchair. This morning, a trunk arrived from Alfynlund, and inside it were several items that I had been unable to bring with me when I departed the Oldlands a week or two ago. Most of these items were souvenirs and other such trinkets I collected during my stay in Valys and Nylanrod, but the one thing that immediately caught my attention was this diary, and I have spent the best part of the morning going over what I had written in it, right up to the day I woke up in a hospital bed. So, you may ask, what exactly happened after that?

Well, as you would expect, the Alfynlundic government instigated an official inquiry into all the events that led up to the night the fire giant escaped from the "Temple of the Mother Tree". As a central figure in these events, I was obviously required to attend this inquiry, where I had to make numerous statements. It was a horrendously tiresome exercise, I must say. But at least it allowed me to get a better understanding of Lord Delmyr's grand scheme.

Lord Delmyr, as it turned out, wanted nothing less than to overthrow the current Alfynlundic ruling class, which he thought of as being corrupt beyond redemption, and replace it with a new one consisting of those who were loyal to the "Order of the Mother Tree", and by extension, to him. However, without the full support of the army, which is of course part of the current ruling class, Lord Delmyr was powerless to act. Thus he conceived the idea of freeing the fire giant, which he would blame on Troluskan agents. The public would demand that the government retaliate, and if the government did not, the military would, inevitably, seize control.

To help him achieve this goal, Lord Delmyr recruited a number of acolytes from the "Order of the Mother Tree", promising them posts in a future Alfynlundic government. This group, which was referred to as the "Hidden Roots", first set about infiltrating several anarchist organisations in Alfynlund, and then instigating those groups to carry out dozens of terrorist acts, both overt and covert. By far the most damaging of these acts were the murders of Crown Prince Uldryc, by bombing, and Lord Galyrod (the former head of the "Order of the Mother Tree"), by poisoning. These men were obstacles to Lord Delmyr, because although, like him, they were both staunch traditionalists, they strongly favoured diplomacy over conflict.

With Lord Galyrod gone, Lord Delmyr had little trouble making sure that he would be elected the next head of the "Order of the Mother Tree", making it much easier for him to advance his plan to release the fire giant. However, there was a big problem. With the royal family also gone, Lord Delmyr needed to find a new heir, and fast. The process of choosing a new heir, when there were no obvious heirs available, was a very slow one, and one that could only take place once the lengthy mourning period for the Royal Family was over. If this process dragged on too long, the "Renewal Ceremony" would have to be delayed for another whole year, and Lord Delmyr was not willing to risk giving the fire that he had stoked any chance of dying down. Therefore, he convinced the Royal Council to expedite the choosing of an heir, arguing that with the threat of war looming ever closer, the public was in desperate need of traditional institutions such as the Monarchy and the "Renewal Ceremony". I'm sure that you are well aware of the events that followed.

My involvement in all this was, in the end, completely coincidental. The inquiry found (as I had long suspected) that there was absolutely no evidence to suggest I had even the tiniest drop of royal blood in my body. Therefore, the Royal Council strongly recommended that I abdicate the throne in favour of a more suitable candidate. I suppose I could have contested the Royal Council's ruling, but to what end? Being Half-Freelander, it seems that from the very outset I was never very popular amongst the people of Alfynlund, and after the incident at the temple, even less so. Some people blamed my incompetence for what had happened. Others even thought that I had been working with Lord Delmyr. In any case, I had never really wanted to be Queen of Alfynlund in the first place, so I agreed to give up the throne, without any hesitation. Consequently, my coronation was nullified, and in my place the young noble who had gone missing a few months earlier, but who had eventually turned up safe in Gomonia, became king. The fire giant, oddly enough, suffered a fate similar to mine. The inquiry managed to convince the public that there was no such creature, cleverly blaming the fire that broke out in the "Temple of the Mother Tree" on an accident with one of the fireworks. The people who had been present during the actual event (including, of course, me) had little choice but to go along with this story, and although there were some who insisted that they had seen a fiery monster on the night of the summer solstice, they were deemed either to have wildly overdeveloped imaginations, or to have been wildly drunk. And Lord Delmyr? He was sentenced to death by the inquiry. Yes, a rather horrible end, but he was a rather horrible person, wasn't he?

After all I've been put through this year, you may be thinking that fate has been rather unkind to me. As Aunt Tilu succinctly put it, I did so much for Alfynlund in such little time, and yet the Royal Council tossed me out like an unwanted, broken doll. But at least they were thoughtful enough to provide me with a generous stipend, which they promised would last as long as I live. Thanks to this money, I will be able to move into a cosy little house nearer to the centre of town (along with my aunt, of course, whose affliction is thankfully in remission). What's more, I'll also be able to afford to study at the University of New Rondir. If you recall, while I was at Nylanrod, it occurred to me that my dance and history lessons would come in useful later in life. Well, now that I have lost the use of my legs, I will never be able to become a dance instructor, but I may be able to become a history teacher.

As important as financial security is, however, it is certainly not the only thing I gained in the Oldlands. I also met and became very good friends with several wonderful individuals, such as Grand Dame Parynfol, Mr Rolinuto, Mrs Lyganol, and even Lady Aralisnova. I treasure the memory of the time I spent together with each of them, and I hope these friendships last a very long time.

Wait one moment. Have I forgotten someone? Oh, that's right. Captain Keldaron! Well, immediately after the inquiry ended, the good captain, who greatly disapproved of the treatment I had received from the Royal Council, magnanimously resigned from the Alfynlundic army. And not only that. He has also decided to leave Alfynlund altogether. It has taken him quite a while to sort out all of his affairs in Valys properly, such as making sure that his dear mother will be well taken care of in his absence, but in the most recent letter I received from him (just two days ago), he informed me that he expects to reach New Rondir sometime early next week. We plan to marry sometime in spring.

www.ingramcontent.com/pod-product-compliance
Lightning Source LLC
Chambersburg PA
CBHW020753130626
46554CB00006B/2171